THE PAPER CLIP
REVOLUTION

BETH LEE
and DEBI CAGLIOSTRO

PAGE PUBLISHING, INC.
Conneaut Lake, PA

First originally published by Page Publishing 2020

ISBN 978-1-6624-1009-3 (pbk)
ISBN 978-1-6624-1010-9 (digital)

Printed in the United States of America

INTRODUCTION

We get to the house. I am simultaneously banging on the door and ringing the bell. Then I add screaming her name to the cadence. I think about kicking in the door like they do in movies. That would be a lot of fun to try. I wonder if I'd break my foot. I wonder if it's really possible, or if it's just one of those things that happen in movies that can never happen in life. Stop it! Stop thinking about action films! Focus!

CHAPTER 1

Day One
First Day of Sentencing

Sam

I hate school. I hate everything about it. I mean everything. I hate it on every sensory level. I hate the overuse of the color beige. I hate the smell of feet and deodorant in the gym. I hate the gray food in the cafeteria that tastes gray. I hate those screaming girls over there who are way too excited about someone's purse. I hate that kid who just bumped in to me. I hate school.

Today is the worst in a series of horrible days. Today earns this distinction because it's the first. The added annoyance today is that all the people who can't normally contain themselves are going to spend the day shrieking about new shoes, new hair, new summer loves, or they are going to wander around lost and worried that they won't find their class because maybe, just maybe, they will be unable to locate room 103, even though it's found next door to 102.

I hate school.

On every other first day, I used to try to convince myself that it was possible this year could be different. Maybe I won't have to sit by Frank who smells like garbage. Or maybe he'd discovered deodorant over the break. Maybe Kaitlyn wouldn't giggle so much and say annoying things like, "Are you so excited about the dance this Friday?"

I don't even pretend anymore. Eighth grade is going to be as horrible as the rest.

I heard there's a new English teacher, someone new to annoy me.

Bri

Yay! It's the first day of school! I absolutely love the first day of school! I can't wait until everyone gets to see my new outfit! I look so cute in this skirt. I love the start of a new year! Everything about it is exciting to me. Who will my teachers be? Who will be in my classes? I just can't wait! I have always loved the first day of school, well, and really, all the days after that. I love the way the school looks when you first walk into it. It's all shiny and bright. I love the calm, cool beige color that seems to coat all the walls. It's so comforting to find that color everywhere I look. Plus that beige wall always brings out my blond highlights whenever I stand near it. I also love that slightly disinfectant smell mixed in with the smell of the new markers, new pens, and new pencils. This is awesome! Everyone is so happy here. Well, almost everyone. Sam is just so miserable. Why does she always look so unhappy?

Who spit in her Cheerios? Well, anyway, I really am excited about this new school year. I tend to do well in all my classes, but my absolute favorite is English. I have always loved English class!

CHAPTER 2

Lunch
The Loud Place with Bad Food

Sam

What a stupid day. All my classes are stupid. I'm not surprised. Now I get to be at stupid lunch.

Look at that stupid kid. Why would you bring a football to lunch? Oh, good. Rachel and Zack are holding hands and looking at each other like the answer to world hunger lies somewhere behind the other's retina. Oh, mother of stupid, the cheerleaders are practicing.

Guess I'll get in line and get some gray. Stupid gray. At least Meg is in line with me. She's not entirely stupid. She's actually pretty tolerable. I hang out with her a lot.

We navigate the stupid traffic and make it to our table. Meg starts telling me about her day so far. It sounds stupid like mine.

Meg and I are on student council together. The meetings go something like this. Meg and I try to impart change at every meeting, but everyone is too concerned about whether we should have Coke or Pepsi at the next stupid dance. Then Meg and I discuss why we show up.

One idea I suggested that was totally not stupid was an adoption day with the local animal shelter. How much would it take to make some posters and show up? The conversation quickly led to the girls saying it would be too sad to see homeless animals, as the guys discussed how cool it would be to see dogs peeing on papers on Mr. Riley's desk. Stupid.

Meg and I show up to volunteer at the shelter on Saturdays now. It's more of a commitment but much quieter.

Meg and I play video games at her house a lot. Sometimes Jack comes. He likes things quiet and not stupid like us. Jack spends the time he's not with us trying to hack in to the school's website. He's obsessed with changing the school's homepage from "Home of the Fighting Cougars" to "Home of the Biting Losers."

As I take a deep breath and prepare to shovel in my "lunch," I become suddenly aware of the sound of a loud *achoo* coming from behind me. This near-deafening noise is followed by a spray of sputum and snot first detected on the back of my neck, then across my cheek, down to my forearm and fork-clenched hand, where it finally comes to rest in my gray. Are you kidding me?

I turn to see who belongs to this stupid, and I see Bri. She is just staring at me unable or unwilling to speak. She never even stops walking past me. Could excuse me, or I'm sorry have been an option?

Bri goes back to her seat. She is sitting next to the cheerleaders who are done practicing. Yay! And the stupid kid with the football. She is a part of the social group that is responsible for making school completely unpleasant.

They travel in packs. This is what gives them power—numbers. When separated, I enjoy how easy it is to unnerve them like, for example, pointing out that they are carrying last season's purse, or telling them that football practice has been canceled. I've also had a lot of fun with a game I like to call "I heard them talking and they said." It always amazes me how quickly they take all information as fact.

If you are ever wondering where to find them, follow the screams. They are celebratory animals. Yay, clothes! Yay, dating! Yay, pizza! Yay, I threw up in my mouth!

The herd is consistently annoying. It is an unintelligent mass of noise and unnecessary joyfulness. They dress the same, act the same, and think the same. I wonder what this week's catchphrase is. Are they done saying "That's totally legit" yet? They care about what to wear and who to sit next to. They overcome life's little tragedies, like clashing accessories, by embracing the knowledge that the right lip gloss can make your day.

And there, in the middle of them all, is Bri, happily unaware.

Bri

Lunchtime. I love the cafeteria because this is the place where I get to see all my friends, and I just get to hang out and talk, without everyone telling me to sit down and stop talking. I sit with my girls. Oh, there they are. They have the best table. There is Jay. He is so cute with his football. He carries his football with him wherever he goes. Rachel and Zack are here too. They make such a cute couple.

I am the head cheerleader, and we always need to practice. There never seems to be enough time for us to practice, so we practice during lunch. It is a good place to practice because there are *so* many kids here to try our cheers out on. Plus it makes everyone happy. Who wouldn't want to hear us cheering during lunch?

I need to get in line to get food. I hope they don't have that gray stuff again. It's way too fattening. I don't even know what is in it! I can't understand what is so difficult about letting us know what is in the gelatinous stuff that is supposed to be food. *Please,* people, have you ever heard of a salad?

So I get on the line with Mandy, my all-time BFF, and while we are waiting, I overhear the terminally unhappy Sam talking to her weird friend, Meg. They are on student council with me and Mandy. They always have these totally depressing ideas of how we should save the whales, puppies, starving children, fireflies, whatever. Why can't student council just be fun without all the serious stuff? Really, don't you think we'll have enough time when we grow up to worry about the planet? Give me a break! I care about the planet as much as anybody else. I have even given up aerosol hairspray even though it works better than the pump. I just think school and, well, basically, life should be fun. I can't stand when people are *so* serious.

Anyway, Sam and Meg were discussing their totally depressing idea of an adoption day at the animal shelter. Um, *hello*, who would want to spend a whole Saturday doing that? We have football games on Saturdays. Some of us have lives.

On my way back to my table, with my hands completely full, I have this uncontrollable urge to sneeze. *Omg*! *Achoo*! And horror of all horrors, I accidentally sneeze on Madame Miserable. Maybe if I pretend it didn't happen, she won't know that it was me! How embarrassing! I wish the floor would open up and swallow me because *she* will never get over this.

Sam is really mean. She is like constantly making up rumors and starting trouble between me and my friends. Why does she need to comment on our clothes and what we do? If she thinks we are *so* stupid, why does she pay attention to us?

At least Jay is sitting over there waiting for me. He always makes me feel better! He is the best boyfriend! I have the greatest group of friends that are always there for me. We have so much in common. We all have the best taste, and we love the hottest looks. Who doesn't like to look their best? The weird, lame, and fashionless ones of the school should really take a lesson from us and maybe even invest in a mirror. It's so obvious that they don't even look in one. Um, did someone tell you that that gross green vomit color matches anything? It doesn't. It's not Halloween.

And there, in the middle of the fashionless, sits Sam.

CHAPTER 3

English Class
Meeting Language Lady

Sam

Last period, finally. I hate this entire stupid day. Okay, here she goes. Hurry up, lady.

She looks normal. She's probably used to be one of the herd. She looks too normal to be interesting. Although that crazy container of paper clips on her desk is definitely not normal. She must have a collection of every possible size and color imaginable. Good to know, in case I have any fastening issues. *Blah, blah,* getting to know each other, *blah, blah,* books.

Okay, language lady, we get it.

Did she just say "Your first assignment is"? *What?* It's the first day. There is no homework. Isn't that a school policy? Isn't it against nature to assign work today? She wants us to write an essay on our favorite color. Seriously?

A piercing screech scrapes through the room. Oh, no, that's just Bri asking how long it should be.

Mrs. Barton said it should be as long as it needed. I may not hate that answer.

She said something like telling someone how long their essay should be was like telling them before it even started that is wasn't theirs anymore. She said everybody's story gets to turn out the way he wants it to. It's like we are in charge or something.

Bri

Last period, finally. This has been a super day, really, but my feet are killing me from these stupid shoes.

At least I get to end the day with my favorite class, English. I have Mrs. Barton. I have heard she is awesome! Plus she has the cutest black pumps on! Anyone with that good taste in shoes must be an awesome teacher. She probably will be *so* fun. *Yay*!

She wants us to write an essay already? Cool, I can do that. It is on my favorite color. That should be easy enough. I asked how long it has to be. Guess who gave me the look of death? Grow up. At least Mrs. Barton gave a pretty cool answer.

Yay! This is going to be so fun!

CHAPTER 4

Color Essays
Mrs. Barton and the Amazing
Technicolor Dream Coat

Sam

Time for first day of school homework! Stupid.

My Favorite Color
Sam Cooper

My favorite color is clear. It is easy to recognize and visible everywhere. It makes me happy when I see it, and I think everyone looks best in it.

Clear can be found no matter where you look. It also doesn't matter what time of day or night it is. Clear is here.

Clear makes me happy because it makes me feel uncluttered and unobstructed. I can really see clear.

I think it is the best color choice for all skin types, and the season never matters. You can't go wrong. It's the clear choice.

Is that going to be too much for language lady on day two? How could she even suggest that knowing someone's favorite color could help us "get to know each other"? Did I say I needed to get to know anybody?

Maybe this sample of my work is better.

My Favorite Color is Plaid
Sam Copper

I love plaid! It reminds me of the clutter and chaos in our lives. Plaid can be loud, like you in the halls. Plaid can be appalling like this assignment.

Let's not forget about all the best plaid things created by Mother Nature herself. Have you watered your plaid plant today? Don't forget Fido and his shiny plaid coat.

Sigh. Okay, fine.

My Favorite Color
Sam Cooper

My favorite color is red. It represents some of my favorite characteristics in myself. It makes me laugh when I see it and reminds me of Christmas.

Red is the color of hostility, fire, and hate. Yeah, I know these aren't the most positive things, but I see them all as qualities of strength that I possess. I think if you have these qualities you can live your life the way you want to. You stand up for what you believe in and command respect. I like being red.

But it really does make me laugh too. I think about the day the devil tries to decide what his signature color will be. Red is the color of a lot of bad stuff—blood, Valentine's Day, cherries. These things all stink. Evil, the Flash, Mars. These things are really cool. Perfect! So he selects fabric, one with a little stretch to it, and sets out to sew his costume. He needs his mom's help on some parts, but he does a pretty good job and is happy with his work. He's going to wear it tonight at the Creatures Who Impact Humans meeting, CWIH for short. Anyway, he shows up ready to wow. He enters the room, strikes a pose, and hears "*Ho, ho, ho!*" Freakin' Santa. He heads home with a heavy heart. He wonders how he can be sinister's poster boy when he looks like an elf. He adds the horns to the hood later that night.

For these reasons, I believe red to be the perfect color.

My Favorite Color
Bri Drew

My favorite color is pink. Pink is the color of everything I love. As a matter of fact, pink is the color of love. Pink has always made me happy for as long as I could remember. I look really good in pink.

Pink is the color of cotton candy and the sand on the beaches of Bermuda. It is the color of sky during a beautiful sunset and the color of a new baby's skin.

Pink is the color of my favorite lip gloss and the color of my Barbie dream car that still sits on my dresser. Pink is the color of my favorite boa from my dance recital when I was three. Pink is the name of my favorite singer.

Pink makes me happy because it is the color of happiness. Everyone's face turns dark pink when they blush. *Pretty in Pink* is one of my favorite old movies.

Pink is practically perfect. I totally love pink, but I don't know if I should turn this in. Madame Miserable would rip me a new one if she saw this. I can hear her now, Pathetically Prissy in Pink. No, thank you. I'll come up with something else.

My Favorite Color
Bri Drew

Red. The most dramatic color there is. Red is the color of everything important. Well, of course, roses are red, Rudolph's nose is red, and obviously, Santa's outfit is red. Papa Smurf's clothing is also red. Little Red Riding Hood is guess what? *Red.* Cardinals are red. These are all really cute things that remind me of being a little girl with pigtails and red ribbons in my hair.

More importantly, some of my favorite foods are red. Watermelon, all dripping down a sunburned face on a summer evening with a red sun in the sky. "Red sky at night, sailor's delight. Red sky in the morning, sailors take warning." My favorite expression my grandfather always said.

Red is the color of Valentine's Day and love. It is the color of confidence and boldness. Picture this if you will. A sleek candy apple red Corvette pulls up in front of a busy office building in the city. A woman in a sexy red power suit, short skirt, cute jacket, and red heels, steps out of the car. She taps her crimson fingernail on her matching lip as if she is contemplating her next conquest. Everyone sees her. How could they not? She will definitely be able to sign the new actor. She is the hottest agent in New York. And all because of the color red. It is the color of my name in lights. Red is the color of my dreams and aspirations.

CHAPTER 5

Day Two
Wrapping and Unwrapping Presents

Sam

It is day two in captivity, and things are still smelly, beige, and loud. I cannot express how badly I would like to go to my locker to throw in every single textbook I had to cover last night. My backpack weighs ninety-seven pounds.

Why do books need covers? Why can't the book's cover be its cover? What, historically, have people been doing to their books to force me to have to protect it from harm? The inside gets by just fine without any protection. Nobody cares about the boogies and crumbs in the pages, but the cover, you have to take care of the cover.

I used dirty-brown grocery store bags to cover my covers.

I throw my books on the lunch table caked with grease and ketchup. Who cares? They're covered. And get in line with Meg.

She tells me absolutely nothing of any importance happened in any of her classes except she has that stupid substitute, Miss Lee. Miss Lee is really annoying. Why is she already here on the second day of school? Meg also said that one girl in her class almost cried because she got a zero for not covering her book. Man, covers have all the power.

I wonder if Mrs. Barton can unlock the secret of the covering. You figure the preservation of books would be a concern of hers since she's all "languagey."

Meg tells me I have to get over the books covers and go to class.

Mrs. Barton collects the essays. She asks us if we are happy with our work. Happy with it? Who cares about happy with it. We are *done* with it. Now, grade it and assign something else. She's looking right at me now, I must be making faces, and asks me if I like what I wrote. I say I didn't know and didn't think about it. So she asks me why I wrote it. *Because you told me to.* What is the confusion here?

Then she says the most profound, ridiculous, stupid, and wonderful thing a teacher could ever say. She says that from now on, if we aren't happy with our work that we can skip that assignment. Wait? Define happy. She wants us to write pieces we are proud of and want to share. She says people write to tell their story when they have something to say. If we aren't proud of it, then we must have left something out, or don't know the ending yet. It's not ready. So instead of getting a bunch of papers with words on them that don't matter to us, and because of that, won't matter to her, we should just wait until the story is ready.

Okay, so I just declare "story not ready" for the year. Great! Even though I had planned out my approach, the rest of the class asked about a million questions. Bri led the class in their cross examination filled with worry and panic. There would be other things to grade us on like grammar and reading comprehension. Any writing assignment completed would be extra credit, and no points would be taken away for the ones we skip. Now shut up and enjoy the gift, people!

I ask Mrs. Barton why we wrote last night's assignment. She says we still had to get to know each other. She sifts through the pages and pulls out the first two essays on the same color she can find. Oh, good, it's Bri's and mine. Mrs. Barton asks us what we have in common. Bri says, "Like, nothing," and I agree. Mrs. Barton reminds us that we both chose red. I would have picked another color if I had known.

She reads my essay first. A bunch of kids laugh when she reads the part I wrote about the devil. They should laugh. It's hysterical.

Mrs. Barton says having a sense of humor is a good quality. Bri mumbles something about how I never crack a smile. Now we have to listen to her stupid essay.

Bri, "the most dramatic 'person' there is," needed to pick my color. Jerk. She should have picked pink to match her stupidity. Red is too cool to be enjoyed by Bri. Poor red is somewhere coloring over itself with yellow to try to be orange. Stupid Bri. Although now I have this great image of the devil's costume being accessorized by red pumps. I should have thought of that.

Mrs. Barton tells us we are starting one of her favorite novels and passes it out. It's called *When I Grew Up*. It doesn't look that long. She also tells us tonight's extra credit essay is *The Event that Changed My Life*.

In order to remove my focus from the unintelligent life forms on the bus, I start the book.

My name is Kevin G. Baker Jr. This is the story about how I grew up. There's some normal stuff to tell you like about my school and friends and homework. But there's some pretty crazy stuff too. I guess I shouldn't go around deciding what's normal and what's crazy. Truth is I really can't tell them apart anymore.

I don't hate this yet. It's nice to enjoy a moment free of stupidity. It won't last. The author probably starts talking about unicorns in the next chapter.

Bri

Day two, and we are already in full swing. It took me forever to wrap my books. I know most people say they "cover" their books. However, I prefer to call it wrap. It really is like wrapping up a present. These books contain gifts. They are like little presents waiting to be unwrapped. I love the whole process: picking out the wrapping paper, wrapping up the books, and making labels with my name and subject on each one. I love it!

The way people cover their books says a lot about them. It's kind of like a great metaphor for how people approach life. I'd like to think if I start with happy books, it can only get better from there.

I never understood people that use paper bags for covers. It's *so* boring and unimaginative. It's like not caring about what you wear to school.

I finally make it to lunch where I share my theory about book wrappers with Jay and Mandy. They think I'm a little obsessed. Maybe, but my books look good.

Mrs. Barton collects the essays. I needed to staple mine, but her stapler is jammed. Mrs. Barton tells me I should use a pretty paper clip because everybody uses staples. She tells me to pick my favorite color. I almost pick up red and then I look up and see her smiling at me. I pick up the pink one. She continues to smile and says she loves pink too.

She asked us the strangest question. She asked us if we were happy with our work. I never thought about that before. About your work being something that you can have happiness with, like a person that you might have a relationship with. Very interesting.

OMG! She just said that from now on, we don't have to do any assignment that we are not happy with. Is she crazy? How will we get graded? How will this prepare me for college? How can we decide what assignments we want to do?

She just said she wants us to write things that we are proud of and want to share. She says people should write to tell their story. If we aren't proud of it, then we must have left something out, or don't know the ending yet. It's not ready. She said we need to wait until the story is ready. What does that mean? I have to ask her.

So I do. I ask, "Will there be other things to grade us on? Will we be doing grammar and reading comprehension? If we decided not to do an assignment because we are not 'happy' with it, will we get an F?"

Nobody else seems worried about this but me.

I am near panic. Mrs. Barton does her best to calm me.

She says we will not be penalized, and any writing assignment completed would be extra credit. This might be one of those little gifts.

Sam then asks one of her typically miserably rude questions. She actually asked why we wrote last night's essay. Mrs. Barton said that we still need to get to know one another. Do I really need to get to know any of these people? I already know the people I want to know.

Mrs. Barton said she was going to read two essays to the class that were on the same color. Great. She just picked mine and Sam's. Apparently, she picked red too. Mrs. Barton asked what we have in common. I immediately said nothing. Sam agreed. At least we agree on something. Mrs. Barton pointed out that we both chose the same color.

I have to admit, Madame Miserable is kind of funny.

Don't get me wrong. Of course, she focused on the hostile side of red, but surprisingly, she wrote about how the devil got his costume. Who knew she had it in her?

Mrs. Barton is like fawning all over her. She said something about how great it is to have a sense of humor. *Sam doesn't ever smile*! She has no sense of humor, no sense of style, basically no sense at all.

Mrs. Barton reads mine to the class. She said she likes the way I associated red with confidence and pointed out the other things that Sam and I have in common. *Please*.

We are going to be reading Mrs. Barton's favorite book. It is called *When I Grew Up*. It looks like it might be a good book.

Tonight's assignment is to write about the event that changed our life the most. I don't think I'll be happy with that.

CHAPTER 6

Home
Cookies and Quiet

Sam

The best part of the day is coming back home. It doesn't sound like something a middle school kid would say, but my house is, actually, great. My mom's there 90 percent of the time. If she's not, she leaves me a note under my snack plate. Yeah, I know. She leaves me a snack. It's just nice.

We usually hang out a few minutes while I eat and tell her about my day. When I was in sixth grade, I was a pretty big jerk to my parents for no reason. When she asked me about my day, I'd just say, "Fine," pick up my food, and leave. What was my problem? I guess I grew up, or raging hormones subsided. Now, I really look forward to telling her stuff.

Today, I got a note that she's at the grocery store underneath a plate of oatmeal cookies and a glass of milk. I'll fill her in on my day later. I decide to start *When I Grew Up.*

My name is Kevin G. Baker Jr. This is the story of how I grew up. There's some normal stuff to tell you like about my school and friends and homework. But there's some pretty crazy stuff too. I guess I shouldn't go around deciding what's normal and what's crazy. Truth is I really can't tell them apart anymore.

My little brother, Mattie, sleeps with his baseball glove. That's crazy. Last April, I ate six worms and a cricket because Doug dared me to. That was crazy. I didn't even get anything for it. My dad's got cancer, and he's sick all the time. That's crazy, but I'm supposed to act normal.

I'm named after my dad and people always tell me I'm just like him. Does that mean I have to get cancer too? Thinking like that's probably normal, I guess.

I can't imagine my dad being sick. I can't imagine him not being here. He's always been really cool to my brother and me. He took us to the opening of the Holocaust museum, Ground Zero. By age ten, I knew about the Trail of Tears and Nelson Mandela. He told us about Greenpeace and first responders. He didn't leave anything out. He wants us to know the world and all its sides. He said the best part about sides is there's usually more than one. He said you can find answers in the sides that aren't right there, out in the front screaming about what they think. He wishes people would see more than just black and white.

My parents never treat us like kids who wouldn't understand. They tell us how it is. They never sugarcoat it.

I wonder where this book is going. If it's Mrs. Barton's favorite, it's got to be for a good reason.

Bri

The house was empty when I got home from school, as usual. Mom doesn't usually get home from work until 7:00 p.m. I called her to check in, but I got her voice mail. Shouldn't she be worried about me checking in?

I figured I'd catch up on my reading for Mrs. Barton's class. I opened up to where I left off.

I came home from school to a strangely quiet house. My mother and father had been away now for over a month. My dad was getting intense chemo treatments and was supposed to be coming home today. Grandma Rose had been staying with us, me and Mattie, and we really missed our old lives. We love having Grandma Rose there and everything. We just miss the way things used to be.

23

I have to admit, I'm a little afraid to see Dad. I really don't know what to expect. When I saw him sitting there in his chair, I was shocked. He did not look like my father. He looked like my Grandpa Jack before he died. He literally looked like a shell of his former self.

What happened to my young, strong father? What would happen to him now?

I had to put the book down for a minute because I knew I was going to cry. But for some reason, I felt compelled to continue reading. I picked it up again.

My mom was standing over my father with a cup. She was trying to get him to drink from a straw. He always loved chocolate shakes. She was speaking to him the way she used to speak to me and Mattie, like she was trying to coax him to drink it. He seemed to hardly understand her.

I stood there watching this scene from some really bad movie. Whose house am I in? How did I get here? What parallel universe is this? I just wished I could go home, to my real home, not this warped one where everything is wrong.

Again, I put the book down. I had tears all over my face, and I hadn't even known I was crying. How did this person explain exactly how I feel in my own house? This is crazy. I am this girl reading this book about this boy, and I feel exactly the same as he does, like a visitor in his own house. How did Mrs. Barton know that I needed this book? How does she know I need to know that I'm not the only one?

CHAPTER 7

Event that Changed My Life Essay
Birth and Bimbos

The Event that Changed My Life
Sam

The event that changed my life is, without question, my birth. I mean, come on, before it, my choices were really limited. Roll, don't roll, stretch, don't stretch. It was also really, really dark until then.

Some things about it were pretty scary at first. I had to come to the realization, quickly, that I had been born into an alien race that was afraid of skin exposure. All them were covered in cloth and wearing masks and hats, even my own father. My mother, obviously a dice roller, chose to forgo the hat, mask, and clothes. Did they think I'd come out spitting? I wish I had.

I remember how bright and cold it was. My natural reaction to this was to scream. Then I suppose to counter the screaming, I was wrapped as tightly as possible in a blanket until I submitted. No one can resist being swaddled. I was placed in my mother's arms. I already admired her for the fact that she was not afraid I'd spit on her.

The aliens greeted me with unintelligible phrases often followed by smelling me and taking my picture. Strange planet.

I kept this day in the forefront of my memories as I vowed, even then, to conquer this race and achieve world domination; therefore, making it the event that changed my life.

Or The Event that Changed My Life
Sam Cooper

My elementary school graduation changed my life. It didn't seem like a big deal while it was happening.

We met at the school for the ceremony. My mom made a really big deal about what I was wearing and how my hair looked. Meg and I hated this but felt resisting was futile. We sat in the gym and listened to our principal tell us how great everything in middle school would be. Jack smiled with anticipation. My mom cried through the entire thing and for the car ride home.

A bunch of my family came over, and I got to invite as many friends as I wanted. This was the best part. I mean, the ceremony was okay, but now my friends and I got to put our normal clothes on and play. Shoes were optional.

We start out playing manhunt in the backyard while we are waiting for everyone to get there. It turns out that we are just running around, chasing fireflies, and getting our feet dirty. Pure joy. Zack tells Rachel that he heard someone liked her. She said she didn't care 'cuz boys were stupid. Mandy and Meg laugh in agreement.

Jack is so happy Jay has arrived with the football. Then Bri comes through the gate.

We played until out parents called us in. We didn't even stop for cake. That was the last day we were all together. After that, everything just changed. Normal clothes turned in to fashionable ones. Shoes became mandatory. Fireflies went unnoticed, followed by snowflakes, clouds, and cartoons.

Do you remember the last time you played? Do you remember the last time you were dirty and didn't care? I do. It was a great day.

The Event that Changed My Life
Bri

An event that really changed my life was the day I was voted head cheerleader. I was always really good. I had been in gymnastics forever. I have always been loud. It seemed natural. I knew that if I was chosen, that would mean that everyone would look up to me. Everyone would look at me as kind of a leader of the school.

Everyone thinks it's always so great to be the leader of the school. And it is in a lot of ways. But it is also a lot of pressure. I can't just wear sweats to school, like ever. Everything I wear has to be a carefully orchestrated outfit. The entire school looks at, no, stares at, what I have on from head to toe. If something is not dead on, people talk about me all day. I hear it in the halls. "*Ew*. What is Bri wearing?"

This is a difficult role to be cast in. But I wonder what would have happened if I was not head cheerleader. Who knows.

Or The Event that Changed My Life
Bri Drew

An event that changed my life. That's easy. It started out as a pretty exciting day. I remember how excited I was because it was our last day of elementary school. I was really looking forward to going to middle school. The graduation ceremony wasn't really that big of a deal, but I was really looking forward to the party at Sam's house. See, we were all still friends then. Before Sam had that permanent scowl tattooed on her face.

We were all outside at her house, Mandy, Meg, Jack, Jay, me, and some others. We were just running around having a great time. It really is the last time I remember us being together like that. That is really the last day I remember really being me, the real Bri, not the Bri that everyone thinks they know.

We had a really fun time. It started to get late, so I figured I had better get home. I was actually surprised that my mom and dad hadn't called Sam's house, or came there to get me. I just went home. When I went into the house, I was surprised by how quiet it was. I mean eerily quiet. Usually when you went into my house, you heard the television blaring. My dad was usually planted in front of it watching any sporting event. In June, it would be the Yankees every night. But not this night. I should have known as soon as I walked in the door that this was wrong.

Did you ever have the feeling that the next thing that happens is going to change your life? I know it sounds crazy, but I felt like I wanted to run because something fundamental was about to change. But, of course, I didn't run. I went upstairs.

I found my mother sitting on the bedroom floor staring at the wall. She wasn't crying. She was just sitting in the dark staring at the wall. I walked in quietly and just stood there. Just then, my father came out of the closet with his suitcase. They both saw me at the same time.

Apparently, they had decided that they would not be married anymore. Apparently, my father was in love with someone else. Someone that is much younger than my mother. Tiffany. What kind of name is Tiffany anyway? It sounds fake, although it goes with her because she is fake too. Everything about her is fake, from her nails to her cheek implants to her chest.

Of course, at the time, I didn't know all this. I didn't know that she would be my stepmother. I didn't know I would have to spend every weekend with her. I didn't know I would have to spend every holiday and vacation with her. I didn't know my parents would constantly be trying to get me to choose sides. I only knew that my life, my family, was destroyed. I knew I would never be the same after seeing that look on my mother's face. I knew I would make sure I would never disappoint her.

It was on that night that I decided that I would only smile. I would make sure my mom would see me smiling. She would see me succeed. She would see me cheer and be happy, and she would think that I was okay.

That is the event that changed everything.

CHAPTER 8

Library
Cupcakes and Control Freaks

"Good morning, Cougars! Happy Thanksgiving Eve! Don't forget to purchase your cupcakes at lunch today! Support your East Shore basketball team by eating some delicious baked goods. Can a custodian please report to the main office? The toilet is not flushing properly," Mr. Riley says on the announcements. "Now please stand for the pledge to the flag."

Sam

Who announces to the entire school that he clogged the toilet? Why is he so annoying? An added annoyance to school has been how cold it's getting. I have to wear a coat and hat, or I'll freeze. Then I have to stuff it into a locker intended for Barbie clothes. Oh, and you're not allowed to wear them. They have to be away. People can get really unnerved if they see coats and hats indoors. I heard it started an international incident once.

What if I wear my robe instead of my coat? And let's just say that my robe has a hood attached to it. Are hooded robes okay? Note to self: check school handbook for loopholes.

Meg thinks I can't wear my robe but is unable to substantiate her instincts. She suggests we bring up scheduling a pajama day at student council. Why don't we have those anymore? Just because you're fourteen, it shouldn't mean you can't be warm and happy at school. Maybe I've got a pair of "feeties" I'd really like to show off. Meg is brilliant.

Meg tells me to stop fantasizing about warmth and get in line. Today is a good day. There's a bake sale. All I heard on the announcements was cheap sugar for sale at lunch. I don't remember whose fundraiser it is. I don't care. I want a cupcake.

Bri and Mandy are in line right in front of us. They're trying to come up with words that rhyme with basketball for new cheers. I'd like to suggest, "Yay, yay, basketball. Your shoes untied, so trip and fall."

I wonder if she ever thinks about how stuff used to be. It doesn't matter. We're on different sides of the fence now.

I believe in healthy eating, don't get me wrong, but sugar and teens are hand in glove. I can see the cupcake I want now. It's a huge chocolate one with chocolate icing and rainbow sprinkles. This is the happiest I've been all year. I reach for it and brush hands with Bri. *No*! It's my delicious mini cake!

Something happens though, and I just decide to not be a jerk. I mean, she was in front of me. Right? I told her to go ahead and take it. I settle for the one next to it. It's vanilla with chocolate icing. No sprinkles. It's time for class.

I actually have to admit that I've been looking forward to English class each day. Mrs. Barton is pretty cool. She seems to like me, a sign of intelligence, even though I haven't turned in one extra-credit essay. She even wrote something I really liked on that red essay I wrote in September. She said she thought I had good ideas. She said I was clever. She said having a sense of humor was one of the best things a person could have. She said she couldn't wait to read more from me.

Okay, so that last part makes me feel pretty crummy. I think I might like to show her some stuff someday but not the whole class. I don't need the world inside my head to see how I tick. They wouldn't get me anyway. I'm not like them. She said we're in charge of our story, right? I'm not sharing. What's the point? Yeah, the assignments have made me think about some stuff, but reading it aloud doesn't solve anything. Nobody would know what I was saying anyway.

When I get to class, there's a sign on the door to meet in the library.

When I get there, I see the class over at the tables. She collects last night's essay and asks me if I have anything to hand in. Of course not.

Mrs. Barton asks us if we know why we need to be quiet in the library. I suggest it is because librarians are control freaks. The actual answer, in Mrs. Barton's opinion, is because every book has something to say. We come here to listen, not talk. Okay, that works for me.

She walks over to the travel section and asks us to raise our hands if we've been to Greece. No hands. She opens the book and stares at it for what seems like an eternity. Someone finally asks her what she's doing. She says she's in Greece and will be back in a minute. We all laugh. She runs shelf to shelf, pausing to go on these "trips" to space, the equator, Kentucky, and back. If we didn't all love her, we'd probably think she was crazy.

Then she asks us to raise our hand if we know how to speak French. No hands. She spends another five minutes grabbing books and teaching herself German and Spanish.

She asks us if we agree that there's a book written on, pretty much, every subject. We all agree. Then she asks if we agree that everyone likes something. She's looking at me, and I laugh. Then she tells us that must mean there's a book for everyone to enjoy.

Then she grabs *Fahrenheit 451*, *Macbeth*, *Lord of the Flies*, and *Catcher in the Rye* and asks us if we've met her friends yet. She takes a deep breath and tells us to look around. She says they're all waiting for us. She assigns the next essay, *Why Do People Tell Stories?*

I walk out of the library in some kind of fog. I'm not sure what has just happened, but I believe I have actually witnessed someone showing me that not only stupid things happen at school. I think I just saw that sometimes, amazing things happen here; things that can reshape the way you think.

Bri

Brr. It is *so* cold outside. There are only a couple of good things about winter: one, skiing; and two, my new ski jacket. Skiing is the one thing that my mom, dad, and I always did together. Every year, without fail, we would go to Colorado for a week-long family trip.

Since the big breakup, my mother won't even think of going skiing. It's like my father got the entire sport in the divorce settlement. If I want to go at all, I have to go with Ski Barbie, a.k.a. Tiffany, and my father.

Because I really am a selfish fourteen-year-old underneath it all, I go. This is seen as an act of treason by my mother. This is the ultimate in *choosing sides.* What kind of people make their child choose sides?

That brings me to the second great thing about winter: my brand-new gorgeous ski jacket. Total guilt present/reward for choosing Dad's side for once. Guess how much my mom loves my new jacket? *Not! Please*, it's a jacket. Get over it, Mom.

I cannot wait to get to lunch today because there is a bake sale for the basketball team, which, of course, I have to support because Jay is, like, the star player. Plus I have been totally craving sugar all day.

I get in line with Mandy, and weird Meg and Sam are behind us. As we were waiting, Mandy and I are trying to come up some new basketball cheers. We really try to keep things fresh. The entire time, Sam and Meg are making stupid little comments. What's up with that? Do I follow them around criticizing their deranged conversations? No, I don't. It is like Sam is on the other side of the world from me. I don't get her.

Oh my god! I have spotted the ultimate cupcake! It is perfectly chocolate with chocolate icing and rainbow sprinkles. Wouldn't you know it? Sam and I reach for the same one at the same time! The most bizarre thing happened though. She actually let me have it. She was actually just human to me. Who knew she even remembered how to be human?

When I get to English class, I saw a sign that says report to the library. I wonder what Mrs. Barton has in store for us today. She really is so fun and *so* creative. She really gets me in ways that most people don't, probably because I do all her extra credit writing assignments. She knows my deepest thoughts.

On one of my essays, she wrote that I was gifted and special. She sees past the cheerleader. She says she loved that I could be so candid about my life. She thinks I'm smart. She says things to me that my mother used to say.

When we got to the library, Mrs. Barton asked us if we knew why we had to be quiet in the library. Sam, who is no longer being a human, had to give some stupid sarcastic answer. Mrs. Barton then gives the greatest answer ever. She says that every book has something to say, that we come here to listen, not talk.

She asks us all these wonderful questions about if we've been to Greece and what languages do we speak, and she literally sits there listening to what the book is telling her. I'll admit, she looks really weird, but it's so effective! I totally get her point. These books all have stories to tell us. Tons and tons of stories are there for us whenever we want them, just like an old friend.

She then grabs a few books and asks us if we've met her friends yet. She says they are waiting for us. I love this crazy, brilliant woman!

Our next essay: *Why Do People Tell Stories?* What a wonderful question. I have a question too. How have I gotten so lucky to finally have someone like Mrs. Barton on my side?

CHAPTER 9

Why Do You People Tell Stories Essays Mini People and Old Ladies

Sam

It's a good thing I'm not turning this in either. I really do not know the answer to this question. Why do people let other people inside their heads? What good does that do anyone? But I can't help thinking about all those books in the library. There was shelf after shelf of people sharing something.

Why Do People Tell Stories?
Sam Cooper

Let's face it. Little kids are loud and weird. They seem to wake up and run full throttle through the world. People tell stories so they shut up and go to sleep. If they didn't, we'd live in a world of zombie grown-ups and crazed mini people.

People also tell stories to annoy me. I don't want to hear about what you did last night, last weekend, or last year. You know what you did, right? So why are you telling me? Oh, and please, do not tell me what you "think." The bigger question is "Why do people annoy me?"

Everyone likes to feel completely exposed, right? I mean, if you do something stupid, you want everyone to laugh at you, or if you do something embarrassing, you hope everyone will see. Oh, and, of course, if you've done something your regret, you want to share it so people can judge you. We could just walk around naked. It's quieter.

Why Do People Tell Stories?
Bri Drew

For as long as there have been people, there have been stories. From way back in the beginning of mankind, when cavemen were drawing on cave walls to Native Americans passing down their stories to modern parents telling stories to their children, people have been telling stories. Why?

People tell stories because they think they have something to say that others might be interested in. Some think they have something to teach. Mostly, they just want to be heard.

An elder from a Tlingit tribe sits with all the young tribe members telling them the stories of the majestic spirit bear. They tell their stories to teach the beauty of this magnificent animal. It is through these stories that the young tribe members learn to respect nature and its beauty. They will remember these stories with great affection to pass on to future generations.

An elderly grandmother sits in an old rocking chair, slowly rocking back and forth. She is surrounded by four generations of family, from her daughter, who is also an old lady, down to her youngest great-grandson. She tells them terrifying stories about her time in Auschwitz and about her escape to Poland.

She tells them of the kindness that some showed her on her escape. She tells them the stories so they know where they came from, yes, but also so they know that in the most horrific events, there is still hope. There is still faith. If it weren't for these people that showed her kindnesses, the ones that took her in, hid her, and gave her food and money, none of them would be here. Not one of the brood that sits at her feet would exist.

She wants the smallest children to remember this and always treat people with respect. She feels it her duty, her obligation, to teach this to her family. She feels this is her opportunity to pay the universe back for the kindnesses that were shown to her.

A mother sits with her small children, reading them *The Little Engine That Could*. She repeats the phrase, "I think I can. I think I can," as the children giggle. She reads them this story every night because it is their favorite, and she wants this phrase engrained in their heads. She wants them to think this in their sleep. She tells them this story because she wants them to succeed in ways she never has.

Books are just stories that are waiting for you. They are full of people sitting around telling wonderful, fantastic, historical, and scary stories. They are waiting for you so they can be told.

CHAPTER 10

English
Developing Stories and a Dumb Project

Sam

I spend the morning annoyed at myself that I forgot to look up the "robe policy." I spent last night stuck inside my head trying to understand why people tell anybody how they feel, what they know, and what they think. It makes me wonder what my story is and what I'm supposed to do with it.

I'm bugging Meg out with the crisis I'm having, so she tells me to stop freaking out and read.

I don't get to do anything I want to do anymore. There's only the stuff I "have to do." I have missed most of my soccer practices because I can't get a ride. When I do get there, I'm late. I tried to bike to one of my games, but when I went in to the garage, I found my bike had a flat. I couldn't find where Dad keeps the pump and Mom wouldn't let me wake him up to ask.

If I was really sick, I could get the cereal I want and maybe even a snack now and then. I'd probably get to go Friday night too. A bunch of the guys are getting together at the movies to see the new Spiderman. *I've been waiting all year for it to come out. It's probably the biggest deal in my life right now, but who cares? I have to babysit Mattie.*

So what? He's sick. Everyone gets sick. It's not like he's going to die or anything. Get up and fix my bike.

This kid, Kevin, is acting like a total loser right now. I mean, his dad is really sick, and he wants to go to the movies and gets mad when he's late to soccer practice. He can't see that things that are bigger than him are happening. He can't see that his dad might die. People die.

Mrs. Barton asks me how I feel about Kevin, and I say he's a selfish jerk. Bri starts freaking out and is defending the jerk, like Kevin's her best friend or something. Why am I surprised? She wouldn't skip a movie date with the herd to do something important. She wouldn't give up anything in her selfish world.

I say I'd give up anything if it were for a good cause. Mrs. Barton smiles and asks me how I know. She asks how I can really know if I haven't been in Kevin's shoes. She says it's a good topic for the next essay and assigns *What would Be Difficult for You to Give Up?* Mrs. Barton tells us she's certain of a lot of things she'd never give up. She says one of them is that she would never give up the opportunity to hear our developing stories.

I wonder if thinking about that will mess with my head too.

Mrs. Barton asks us if we think Kevin is acting grown-up. No, he's acting like a dumb kid. Mrs. Barton asks if grown-ups are ever dumb. I say absolutely and try to tell her how dumb my other teachers are, but she won't let me finish. Then she tells us we have to do a group project. We have to research another culture and answer the question: When are you considered grown up?

That's probably pretty easy. Looking stuff up is no big deal. I just hate it that it's a group project. Why would Mrs. Barton do that to me?

She starts breaking us into groups and puts me with Bri. What, cosmically, have I done wrong to deserve this? I look up at Mrs. Barton, then at Bri who quickly turns away. I'd rather eat bugs off monkeys.

Bri

We had a reading assignment last night. The part we read was about how Kevin, the protagonist, feels he can't do anything anymore. He feels that whatever he wants is secondary to what the family needs or wants. He wants to go see *Spiderman*, but he can't because he has to babysit his brother. He is late for soccer practice because no one is there to take him.

Mrs. Barton asks us how we feel about Kevin and the way he is behaving. Sam answers in her typical way that she answers every question. Of course, she thinks Kevin is a jerk. She says he is selfish. Really? Selfish? I really would like to point out to her that *one* thing Kevin is not is *selfish*. He is, however, something that Sam isn't. He is human. He is dealing with something that is beyond his scope of understanding, and all he knows is how his life has changed.

I can so relate to Kevin. I can relate to him so much that it actually physically hurts. How could Sam ever understand something like this? Her family is practically perfect. Her parents do *everything* for her to make her life easier. Her mother used to leave her cute little snacks and write little notes to her every day. I wonder if she still does that.

I don't point any of that out, though. Instead, I timidly raise my hand. I say that Kevin is not selfish. He is fourteen. Therefore, it is not his responsibility to think of the whole family. It is not his responsibility to take care of Mattie. It *is* his responsibility to go to school, get good grades, and play soccer. He is supposed to be a child, not an adult. It is unfair and even a bit inappropriate to expect children to handle, or deal with problems like adults. They are not adults.

After my little tirade, I just stop talking. I probably said too much. Nobody seems to know what to say. Mrs. Barton thinks for a minute. (Another thing I love about her. She doesn't just blurt things out. She always thinks before she speaks.) She then says sometimes you have to give things up. That's it. Just sometimes, you have to give things up. It's so simple. It's perfect.

Again, Sam starts with this she would give up anything for any good cause. *Oh please.* What has she ever had to give up? Are you kidding, Sam? Is it possible that you are really that clueless?

Mrs. Barton is ready for her. She says, "How do you know?" She asks her if she has ever had to give anything up. Take that, Madame

Miserable! Mrs. Barton is like a superhero sent here to fight the know-it-all judgmental miserable people of the school!

Mrs. Barton then assigns our next essay, *What would Be Difficult for You to Give Up?* I could write volumes on this one.

Mrs. Barton tells us she would never give up listening to our developing stories. I like that idea. We are all really just developing stories.

She asks if we think Kevin is acting like a grown-up. As I said before, um, no, and he shouldn't. She says we are going to be doing group projects on *What Makes Someone a Grown-up?* in another culture. That sounds pretty interesting and not too hard.

Kill me now. She just assigned me to work with Sam.

Sam and Bri

She can't be serious. I go up to her desk the second class is over. Bri's right behind me. There's no reason to dance around this. Bri's up there for the same reason, so I just blurt this out.

"Mrs. Barton, wait, I can do this research myself. I don't need a partner."

"Mrs. Barton," Bri pleaded, "really, you have no idea how difficult she is to get along with. There is no way I can work with her, or even deal with her. This will be a complete—"

"Come on, please. We can't work together," Sam interrupted.

"How do you know? When I selected the groups I thought you two were the most natural pair."

"We won't even be able to agree on a topic because Sam and I have nothing in common at all," Bri countered.

"Then you don't see what I see. When you don't see things the same, it is not a curse, it's a gift. So many people's great ideas get blocked by some wall they can't climb over. Having someone already on the other side makes it easy for these great ideas to grow into great things. You just open your mind and listen as they tell you what it's like over there. They can help you see what you didn't think you could. I'm just asking you to remember what words are for. We use them to communicate. What you have to say is up to you, but the more you communicate, the more you understand. The more you understand, the better your story gets. If you take your story to the other side of that wall, that place you only heard about, your story grows and grows until it gets so big, it reaches another wall. But you just keep finding someone on the other side." Mrs. Barton took a deep breath and then continued, "Ladies, this is just a wall. Instead of spending your energy focused on how this wall was built, spend some time listening to the other side. Trust me. You might be surprised about what is on the other side."

With that, Bri obnoxiously says, "Okay, Mrs. Barton. We'll try."

I guess that's it. Bri is coming over.

CHAPTER 11

What would Be Difficult to Give Up Essays Ice Cream and Apple

What would Be Difficult to Give Up
Sam Cooper

What a world we live in. You can turn the news on, pick up the paper, and learn about people from a block away to a continent away hurting every day. How are you supposed to process that?

The most frustrating part is I can't do anything about it. I'm just a kid. All I can do is try to organize coat drives and animal adoptions. Come on! What's that helping? How is everyone on a different side?

People wonder why I'm miserable. Should I cheer when people are starving? Should I plan my next outfit when soldiers patrol a boarder? Maybe I should touch up my makeup while some crazy guy shoots up a Wawa because they're out of Cherry Garcia.

Middle school doesn't matter. The world does. Until I'm out there making a difference, the thing I would find most difficult to give up is my sarcasm.

What would Be Difficult to Give Up?
Bri Drew

What would be incredibly difficult to give up? My iPhone.

I know. It's shocking. A teenager that doesn't want to give up her phone. Yeah, of course, there are all the usual reasons. I need it to keep in touch with my friends, and I need it for my iPod. *Blah, blah, blah.* How many fourteen-year-old girls would write the same exact thing?

But here's the thing. I am sitting here in my room on my bed trying to think of something else that would be hard to give up. I kind of already gave up my relationship with my parents, or at least the way my parents used to be, and, let me tell you, it's difficult.

I already gave up family holidays. I gave up family vacations and kissing my dad good night. I really feel that I have given up so many things and that they all have been very difficult.

So why do I need my phone? I need it because it makes things less difficult. It makes it less difficult to get in touch with my father, or for him to get in touch with me. It makes it less difficult for my mother to find me when she needs me.

It wouldn't be difficult to give my phone for the usual teenage reasons. It would be difficult to hold on to what is left of my family if I had to give up my phone.

CHAPTER 12

Sam's House
Soccer and Secrets

Sam

A perfectly good Saturday, ruined. I can't believe she's coming to my house. I'm supposed to be watching *Justice League* and eating Cheerios.

One-and-a-half hours until impact. Time to set the stage. If I bring her in through the garage, we could work right in the family room. Of course, she might be too comfortable in there, too relaxed. I want her to hurry up and get out. I'd also completely freak out if she sat in my spot, or got Bri all over the remote.

If she comes through the front door, it's about twenty paces to the kitchen table. Come on. I have to eat in there. We are setting up in the living room. No one ever goes in there. It's filled with Mom's furniture she doesn't like people to sit on. That room could smell like Bri for a week, and I'd never know.

I set up the laptop, grab my English notebook, and wait. I start imagining what it's like on the "other side of the wall." First, I picture unicorns eating cotton candy.

Bri

Well, here I am on my way over Sam's house. My mom had to take me early because she supposedly has to work today. She is talking incessantly about how great it is that Sam and I are getting together after all these years. I have told her too many times to count that we are not friends again. We have to work together on a project. That's it. She doesn't seem to hear this. Actually, she doesn't seem to hear a lot of what I say.

She is going on and on about how cute we both were when we were like five years old. We used to be on the same soccer team. My dad and Sam's dad were the coaches. We thought that made us really cool. We loved calling our dads "Coach Daddy." What happened to that Sam? What made her become this completely different person, and how am I supposed to spend the day at her house?

When I got there, it seemed pretty strange. Sam met me at the door almost immediately, just like she was standing by the door, waiting to let me in. The living room looked exactly the way it used to. I felt like I was a little kid again.

Sam led me directly to the living room where she had everything set up, like a strange little office.

Sam and Bri

"Sit. Do you want a Coke?" Sam asks.

"No, I'm fine."

"Bri, please ask if I have Pepsi."

"Do you have any Pepsi?" Bri asks.

"No. Water?"

"Really, I don't want anything. Can we just get on with this? I'd rather not be here all day," Bri says.

"Do you want to just start googling?" Sam asks.

"The librarian told us to use Expert Space, but sure. Why don't you just type in *When Are You Considered Grown-up?*" Bri says.

Sam types in *When Are You Considered Grown-up?* and sees pages of info. Bri grabs the first one she thinks is super neat—Gaelic Games.

"You know what this reminds me of? I was actually thinking about it on the way over! Do you remember when we played soccer?" Bri asks.

"Yeah, I remember playing soccer. I'm not old. It was fun," Sam admits.

"We used to run like we thought we were so fast. Remember, we thought we could run faster than our dads. They would always pretend we were too fast for them. You really had fun," Bri says.

"Yeah. I did. We were a bunch of little kids running around. No matter what happened we went out for ice cream. Yeah, soccer was fun."

"Remember that day I scored a goal, and we were so excited and jumping up and down until we realized that I scored on our own team! It was so funny!" Bri laughs.

Sam laughs at the memory.

"I still have that dumb trophy," Sam says. "Can you believe it?"

"You do? I wouldn't think you would be the sentimental type," Bri says.

"I just kept the trophy. I'm not all gooey about it. Hey, this one's great, Debutante Ball. Young women are 'displayed' to eligible bachelors. I can't believe we still have these. It sounds like a dog show. What do the guys just get to pick the one they like? There's one in New York, Bri, you should go."

"It would be super cool to get to pick out a really awesome dress and have this great party," Bri says.

"How can we live in this century and still have customs like this? I wonder if they feel stupid about themselves, or get really excited they get to debut. Maybe they just do it because their parents tell them to," Sam says.

Bri adds, "I like the idea of being a 'female beginner.' It's just the coming out part that I have a problem with. Coming out of what? Hey! Here's one! The Cherokee Rite of Passage. It even sounds cool."

"Wow, that's great. They have to stay in the woods on a tree stump, blindfolded, all night. I give credit to the guy who made up blindfolded. That's just funny. I know some people who could really benefit from this rite of passage," Sam says.

"Let's make a list. Number one, Mr. Riley. Maybe if they had done that when he was younger, he wouldn't be such a loser now. How about Kaitlyn? Nobody would miss her! Or that weird kid, Michael Delnick! Definitely him," Bri blurts out.

"I have to admit, Meg could use a few hours, maybe not the whole night. And it wouldn't be so bad to send Mandy with her. They could worry about starvation and being eaten alive by mosquitoes," Sam adds.

Sam is struck by the fact that they are both laughing at the idea of sending half our school's student body into the woods to learn. She hasn't laughed this hard in a long time, and she can't believe it's with Bri.

"Hey, really, do you want a soda? We have all kinds of stuff. Pepsi too? And my mom made cookies."

"Sure, that would be great. Are you sure *you* didn't make the cookies? I'm a little concerned about you poisoning me," Bri jokes.

"I'll be right back," Sam says.

Sam thinks Bri's actually not as annoying as she used to be. She recalls how much fun they had and wonders what happened that everything just changed. She can't even remember why she's mad anymore.

Bri

I can't believe Sam still has the trophy. I wonder where she keeps it. I get up and started walking around, just taking things in. Like I said, I spent a lot of time here when I was younger. As I'm walking down the hall, I'm drawn into Sam's room. I walk in. Yup, there's the trophy, right on her desk. Who would have thought she would have saved the trophy after all these years? She acts like she doesn't care about anything.

As I am standing there in her room looking at the trophy, I find the most amazing picture. It's of that day, that day that my life changed. It's the one that Sam's mom took at the graduation party. It's a picture of all us, the whole gang: Sam, K, and me with our arms around each other with these goofy grins. We're so young in the picture, but that is not the amazing part of the picture. The amazing part is that Sam still has it.

I put the picture down and find this huge folder. It says "Barton Essays" across the top. I know I shouldn't pick this up, but I have to. I can't not open it. The folder is full of all the essays we have written since the beginning of the year. She has never turned any in. I thought she just hadn't done any.

I open the folder and start reading *The Event that Changed My Life*. She is talking about her birth. She actually wrote an essay about how her birth changed her life! This is *so* funny. Why wouldn't she turn these in?

I turn to the next one and begin reading. This one is also titled The Event That Changed My Life Sam Cooper.

My elementary school graduation changed my life. It didn't seem like a big deal while it was happening.

We met at the school for the ceremony. My mom made a really big deal about what I was wearing and how my hair looked. Meg and I hated this but felt resisting was futile. We sat in the gym and listened to our principal tell us how great everything in middle school would be. Jack smiled with anticipation. My mom cried through the entire thing and for the car ride home.

A bunch of my family came over, and I got to invite as many friends as I wanted. This was the best part. I mean, the ceremony was okay, but now my friends and I got to put our normal clothes on and play. Shoes were optional.

We start out playing manhunt in the backyard while we are waiting for everyone to get there. It turns out that we are just running around, chasing fireflies, and getting our feet dirty. Pure joy. Zack tells Rachel that he heard someone liked her. She said she didn't care 'cause boys were stupid. Mandy and Meg laugh in agreement.

Jack is so happy Jay has arrived with the football. Then Bri comes through the gate.

We played until out parents called us in. We didn't even stop for cake. That was the last day we were all together. After that, everything just changed. Normal clothes turned in to fashionable ones. Shoes became mandatory. Fireflies went unnoticed, followed by snowflakes, clouds, and cartoons.

Do you remember the last time you played? Do you remember the last time you were dirty and didn't care? I do. It was a great day.

I stood there staring at the paper. I couldn't believe what I was reading. My head was actually spinning. Her day that changed her life is the same as mine? She cares that we're not friends anymore? Just as I was trying to process all this, to make sense of any of it, Sam walked in the room.

Sam and Bri

"What are you doing in here?" What are you doing with those?"

Sam rips the folder out of Bri's hands. Sam can't even begin to process that *she* is in her room. *She* is reading the very things that weren't meant for *anyone* to see.

"Sam," Bri tries to speak but is still having difficulty believing what she just read. "Those are really good. I can't believe how well you write."

"I don't care what you think of them, Bri. They aren't yours to read and reflect on. How could you do that?" Sam shouted.

Bri, almost crying, says, "I didn't mean to. I was just walking down the hall, and I saw the door open. Why don't you turn them in? They are *so* good. You are really funny."

Sam fumes, "I don't want the world in my head, Bri. I don't need anybody creeping around inside my thoughts trying to understand what makes me, me. You want to take some guesses, go ahead. But you'll guess wrong. I'm not 'Madam Miserable' for no reason. Yeah, I know what you call me. When did you start thinking I was such a freak? So what if I don't get your stupid school spirit. There's a whole world out there beyond cheering. And you know what, Bri?

It's a really sad place. I didn't turn these in because I'm not 'happy' with my story. Maybe if I could just go to a pep rally, I'd be cured. I'm not like you, Bri. I wish I was. It would be nice not to care about anything important."

Sam crosses over to stare out the window. She tries to take a deep breath. She's scared she'll bawl like a dumb baby. She can't let Bri see her break down.

"You need to leave," Sam snaps.

"You can't control people's reactions and who really cares if it's different from what you thought they should think. You might learn something new. And I hate to be the voice of reason here, but we need to finish this project, regardless of what you think of me," Bri retorted.

"Fine. I'll be over tomorrow at twelve."

"Fine. Did it ever dawn on you that perhaps there is a reason why I surround myself with pep rallies and things like that, or are you just too busy looking at things from your side? You know what? Don't answer me. See you tomorrow."

With that Bri quickly grabs her things and walks out of the house.

CHAPTER 13

Bri's House
Dressed to Kill with Jazz Hands

Bri

Yesterday was going really great until Sam saw me in her room. She completely freaked out. Now she is coming here. We just need to get this project done, so we can bring it to Mrs. Barton. I don't think Mrs. Barton really knows how far back this thing with Sam goes. I can't believe that Sam still thinks about the old days. I never knew she would even acknowledge that we used to be friends. I never thought about her side. That's what I am struggling to understand. What exactly is Sam's side? That everything sucks? If you think that everything sucks, how can *anything be fun?* She has everything. How can she think she has nothing? I just need to get this thing over with.

Sam

Yesterday was a nightmare. It took me a while to come away from the window. So Bri doesn't get me. Shocker. She actually didn't understand that I was totally freaked out that she was in my room touching everything I own. So what that I liked being a kid. So what that I miss the days when life was easier. You go from being this happy kid to middle school. We are old enough to know more about our world but too young to change it. We are old enough to stay home alone but too young to want to. We are old enough to go to the park whenever we want but don't have any time to "play." It's like the place you wait until you're old enough for your life to start. Maybe you're supposed to spend it at stupid football games. It would be a lot easier to be like Bri. She doesn't have to worry about anything except cute shoes. Must be nice.

Bri

Well, I'm going to beat her at her own controlling game. I will set up my own little demented work space. Sam totally hates pink, so I will make the whole area pink!

I decided that I would use the living room too. I put pink pillows on the couch and took out my Hello Kitty laptop cover from the bottom of my closet and shoved it on the computer. I got my pink notebook paper and pink gel pens. I even took out the pink paper clips. It was enough pink to even make me feel sick, like Pepto-Bismol spilled all over the place. What's that they say? You have to be able to laugh at yourself, right?

Sam

I prepare for battle. I decide I'm not showing up without armor. I begin with black jeans and a black T-shirt. I ask Mom if I can borrow her weird old biker jacket. I'm glad she used to be cool. I really need this prop. I finish the look with my Doc Martens and some black eyeliner. My mom asks if it's Halloween. Success. I ask my mom to put loud music on for the car ride over. So maybe it was the *Hairspray* soundtrack.

Bri

Sam is supposed to be coming over at 12:00 p.m., and I was hoping that my mom would be out of the house by now, but she must be having one of those days because she is not getting out of bed. She does that sometimes, just stays in bed all day.

Sam and Bri

Bri met Sam at the door because she didn't want Sam to ring the doorbell.

"Hi, let's just get this over with," Bri says.

"Why did you meet me at the door? Were you afraid someone would see me here?" Sam asks.

"Um, no, actually, I didn't want you to ring the bell. My mom is sleeping."

"Really? It's twelve. Why is she still sleeping? Is there something wrong with her?" Sam asks.

"She stays in bed a lot since my dad left. What are you wearing?" Bri asks.

They walked into the living room. Sam notices that things aren't as nice as they used to be. Bri notices her looking around.

"Sam, I know it doesn't look that great in here. My dad used to take care of all these things," Bri says with a wave of her hand, "and I think my mom has really just kind of given up. Let's just work on the project, okay?"

"Okay, it will take my mind off the pink."

"Do you want to do debutante ball?" Bri asks.

"Yeah, it will be easiest for us," Sam says.

When Are You Considered Grown Up?
Bri Drew and Sam Cooper

Many cultures around the world mark what they consider the growth of their children into adulthood. It can be marked by physical age or emotional maturity. Cultures celebrate this new adulthood with a celebration. One such celebration is a debutante ball.

A debutante is a young girl, between the ages of fifteen to eighteen with an upper-class family. Balls are held all over the world and are intended to display the girl to her community for having reached an age where she is eligible for dating or marriage and has completed both academic and social studies. The girls are also duty bound to uphold the traditions of the ball itself like learning ballroom dance and proper etiquette.

One tradition is the girls wear white short-sleeved dresses with white gloves and a train.

We chose the debutante ball because it annoys us on many levels. First, why is this stupid dance limited to rich people? Poor people grow up too. Why can't they show up in their dumb white dress and not talk with their mouths full? We also think it's completely barbaric that in this century, we would display anybody for anything. Displaying young girls like they are objects is disgusting.

"Delete the last paragraph," Bri says.

Sam sighs. "Fine."

We chose the debutante ball because we think it is interesting that a tradition that may seem antiquated has survived to present day. We would love to know what it's like to have the honor of being a "deb" and can only guess how great the sense of pride is that the girls must feel.

"Is this stupid enough?" Sam asks.

"It's fine. It's done," Bri says.

"I'm not really 'happy' with this, Bri. Why can't we just throw it out, or I could put it in my folder of secrets?" Sam asks. "Oh, wait, it's not secret anymore."

"Let it go. This one's an assignment. We did what she asked us."

Bri clicks print and start cleaning up the area. In some temporary moment of insanity, Bri thinks she's with a human and asks, "What do you think makes you grown up?"

"I used to think it was when I got my big-girl pants. But really, I just think my mom was sick of buying diapers," Sam says.

What did Bri expect? "Come on, really?"

"You're grown up when you put someone else before you. That can happen when you're ten or forty. It's when you stop being selfish," Sam says. "Why?"

"I was just wondering what you thought. I mean you seem like you're in such a rush to be an adult. I was wondering what you thought was so great about it. It all just looks sort of lonely and disappointing to me," Bri says.

"Being an adult and being grown-up are totally different things, but maybe it's the idea that you can make it whatever you want it to be instead of just being told what you have to do. Now, can you please explain to me why you have unopened presents over there?"

"The presents are Christmas presents for my dad. Get that look off your face. I know it's February. He and my wicked stepmother-to-be are skiing. Who knows when they'll be back."

Great, Sam's actually speechless over how sad that is.

"So, do you want to turn this in early to show her we got it done?" Sam suggests.

"Yeah, meet me at lockers in the morning. We'll go straight to her," Bri replies.

CHAPTER 14

School
A Bad Story

Sam

I hated Bri's house. I can't get over how different it looks. It was always so perfect. Now it looks, sort of, worn. You'd never know it by looking at Bri, but I guess it must be pretty tough without her dad. I have to say it didn't smell that great in there either. It wasn't gross or anything, but it was stagnant air. It used to smell fresh, like flowers and cookies and perfume. It used to smell like life. The soda Bri gave me was flat. I guess no one had been to the store in a while and then there was the eerie quiet. Why was her mom in bed at noon? I left around 2 p.m. and never saw her. I don't know how Bri holds it together. It's like she's alone. I'm kind of touched by the fact that she walks around smiling.

Bri

I still don't get why Sam hates her life so much. I mean I get why she is sad. But *miserable*? I loved being at her house, for just a few hours. It was like, I don't know, cozy. It even smells nice in her house. It smells fresh. My house smells dead. How can a person that has parents *and* cookies be so miserable? What is wrong with her?

Sam

Why did I agree to meeting in the locker section? It's like being in Tokyo. Layer after layer of kid is trying to get next to, behind, between, beneath, and above. Ridiculous. There's always some guy just standing there, too, right in the way. He's done. He's got all his crud. He's just standing there now. I live in fear of being trampled to death right here in front of my locker. I'd be left here to rot for days. You'd never find me. Everyone has to drop their stuff all over the floor. Pencils, homework, candy, gum wrappers, books, and gym clothes. Why do we have lockers if people just throw their stuff on the floor? The smell would eventually give away my location.

Bri

I can't believe that Sam actually says that she wanted to meet me at her locker. She probably feels sorry for me after being at my house. Great. That's all I need—pity from Sam.

Sam and Bri

Here comes Bri. "Hey, was your bus late too?"

"Yeah," Bri says, "all the buses were late. You know, Jay's dad is a cop, right?"

"No. Who cares?" Sam asks.

"Jay said his dad got called to the accident that blocked traffic on our way in. He said it was bad."

"I thought it was the rain. It's pouring out. Then I saw all the flashing lights. It looked like there were a lot of emergency vehicles. Crazy. Are you ready to go see her?" Sam asks.

"Yup, let's go," Bri responds.

"Do you think she'll be surprised we finished?" Sam asks.

"No, I think she knew we could do it. That's why she put us together in the first place," Bri says.

Bri notices Sam is carrying her Barton essay folder.

"Are you handing those in?" Bri asks.

"When do you stop spying?" Sam snaps.

As we get closer, we see Mr. Riley is at her door. I wonder what he's doing here. He's talking to some lady. I think she's a sub. I've seen her around the building. I look at Bri. She looks confused too. I prepare myself to speak like a normal well-adjusted model citizen of East Shore Middle School.

"Good morning, sir. Excuse us. We need to see Mrs. Barton." I sound totally normal.

Bri is laughing at my performance. We walk right past them and into Mrs. Barton's room, but she isn't there. Mr. Riley has followed us in with the lady.

"Mr. Riley, is she absent today?" Bri asks. The pause is forever. "Mr. Riley?" He's looking down at the floor, then up to the ceiling, then back at the floor again.

Finally, he takes a deep breath and speaks. "Bri, Sam, this is Miss Lee. She's going to be covering Mrs. Barton's classes. We just got word that Mrs. Barton was involved in that accident outside on Cougar Lane. She was pronounced dead at the scene."

Bri runs to the window. Flashing lights are still visible in the distance.

Sam runs out of the room clutching her Barton essay folder.

CHAPTER 15

Reality
Bri's New Soundtrack

Bri

I stand there, for I don't know how long. I can't make myself move away from the window. I see the lights flashing, and they seem to have me under some kind of strange spell. I think Mr. Riley says that Mrs. Barton died in the accident. The very accident that is outside. How can that be?

Please let this be a dream. Please let this be a dream. Please let this be a dream. I repeat this over and over on my head. It has become some kind of demented chorus to a song I can't get out of my head. Please let this be a dream. I can tell there is something going on in the room around me, but I don't know what. It all seems separate from me. I'm not really part of anything going on. I'm just standing at the window. I hear muffled voices, "Terrible tragedy," "What a loss," and "Her poor family." Please let this be a dream.

Someone comes and grabs my arm. They lead me to my home-room. As I am walking, floating down the hall (Is it walking if you have no recollection of your feet touching the floor?), I continue to hear little bits of that awful conversation.

"Who will replace her?"

"Miss Lee."

I keep walking. I hear some laughter. People are laughing?

People are laughing *today*? I can't believe anything can be funny today, *now*, when there is an ambulance outside the window with Mrs. Barton in it. With Mrs. Barton gone. How can there be laughing?

Mr. Riley comes on the announcements. I am barely listening to him, but somehow, I hear Mrs. Barton's name. He is talking about her. He says something about how she will be sorely missed. Really, you think so? What a dumb thing to say. Although, what wouldn't be a dumb thing to say? Somehow I get through homeroom, math, and science. The whole morning seems to go by in a blur. It's like I'm sitting in a car with my head against the window. Everything is speeding past me. Somehow it's lunchtime.

I just walk in the cafeteria and sit at our usual table. There seems to be a lot of crying in here. It's strange because it's not everywhere. There's some people going on like normal and then there are these clusters of people crying. There also seems to be various degrees of crying. Some, just tears in their eyes. Some are sobbing. Some seem to just be caught up in the drama of it all.

There are counselors everywhere. What did they import them from other schools? I sit at a table. It doesn't even occur to me to get food. You don't have to get lunch in a dream, and I am sure that I will be waking up any minute now. So I sit. Jay seems to be talking to me. I can't hear him. I can't even focus on what he is saying. I wonder where Sam is. I don't think I've seen her in a while.

Lunch is over. More crying. More counselors. I think one of the counselors is talking to me. I walk into Mrs. Barton's class, and it's all too much. Everyone is crying. More counselors, and the dream is still going on. I realize that I am still singing that *Please Let This Be a Dream*-song. I can't stay here. I can't do this. I feel like I am suffocating or drowning or something. I only know I can't stay here.

So instead of sitting in my seat, I turn around. I walk down the hall and out the side door. I walk down the sidewalk. I am vaguely aware that I shouldn't just leave school, but I don't seem to be controlling my movements. I find myself standing at the spot where it all happened. The spot where I lost the only person that really understood me. The spot where I lost the only person that saw me for something other than the dopey cheerleader.

I notice all these flowers, stuffed animals, candles, and pictures all over the ground on the spot. Why? Does this help people? If it helps, maybe I should leave something. I realize I don't have anything. I don't even have my coat. I hear this strange buzzing. What is that? It's coming from my pocket. It's my phone. I look at it. It says, "Jay calling."

I throw the phone on the pile of stuff on the spot. Maybe it will help. I start walking. I walk all the way home. I go in the front door and shut it. I stand in the foyer leaning on the front door and seem to slide down the door until I am sitting on the floor. I notice that the floor is soaking wet. How did the floor get so wet? Then I realize it's from me. I am soaking wet. I am soaking wet with my knees pulled up to my chest, and I am shivering.

Somehow I have gotten myself home from school, but now, I need to get to my bedroom. I don't think I can do it. It may as well be across the world because I can't take another step. So I don't. I lie down on the floor in my wet clothes and listen to *Please Let This Be a Dream*-song until I fall asleep.

CHAPTER 16

Reality
Sam's Sorrow and the Idiot

Sam

When I woke up this morning, I forgot. For about three seconds, I forgot I was broken. Then I remembered, and I felt the pain sting me again.

When I ran out of the room yesterday, I didn't know where I was going. I just knew I couldn't stay there. Mr. Riley was doing the announcements telling us it was February 28 and that driving to school in the morning can kill you. I ran down the stairs, past our lockers and out into the parking lot. Red lights were still flashing. I turned and ran out toward the field. I was soaking wet by now but didn't care. I was probably cold but couldn't tell. All I knew was my legs couldn't carry me anymore. I collapsed in the grass and pulled out my phone.

"Mom, can you come get me?"

I wasn't able to get out much more than that. Once I started crying, I couldn't stop. She pulled up about ten minutes later. She got as close to the field as she could, parked, and came out to get me. I was glued there.

When we got home, she made me change into dry clothes. She said I was shivering uncontrollably. I did what she said, but the cold inside never went away. She stayed with me all day.

My mom said I could stay home today, but I want to go to school.

As the bus passes by the accident scene, you can see that people have started a makeshift memorial. There are flowers and candles and stuffed animals. I wonder if it helps you feel better. I'll try anything.

I didn't notice Bri at lockers, so I check for her again at lunch. I see Mandy at the table and Jay, but she's not there.

Meg starts telling me how everyone cried all day yesterday. Everyone was a mess. Bri must have hated seeing everyone upset. Meg asks me about my mental breakdown yesterday. It's funny that she thinks it's over. I tell her she'd understand if Mrs. Barton was her teacher, but I don't say her name to Meg. I just say "she" because I know I'll cry if I say it. I'm glad lunch is over.

Miss Lee starts class. She says she didn't do any work yesterday "due to certain events." Events! Events! What could it be? Oh yeah, best person in the world died, right? It wasn't so much "events" as just a plain old "event." I mean, dying is a singular event, and you really don't need to surround it by other events. It's a stand-alone thing. Not a good start, sub.

Michael asks if she would like to collect our group project and mentions some of us may have extra-credit essays to turn in. She says no. She says she wants to start fresh. She says she's not Mrs. Barton, and things are going to be different now. She says she wants us to *forget* the first half of the year and begin from today. Where did they get her from?

I consider raising my hand to discuss my inability to *forget*, or maybe suggest that she let me throw every eraser I can find at her in order to start fresh tomorrow instead. I'd also really like to write "idiot" on her forehead with a sharpie, again, before the new beginning.

She asks us to pass forward *When I Grew Up*. What? She says we won't be reading it anymore. But we didn't finish.

Everyone else starts passing it forward like the lemmings they are. I feel like I'm going to scream or cry or both, so I raise my hand and ask if I can go to guidance. She can tell I'm upset but has no clue why. She signs my pass, and I'm gone before she can ask about my book.

I'm walking as fast as I can to get away from there, but I really don't know where I am going again. I don't really want to go to guidance. Mrs. Johnson will try to reference one of the posters on her wall with a dumb phrase on it and usually a kitten. This is not a hang-in-there occasion.

I go in to the first girls' room I see and lock myself in the stall.

I want to cry, but I'm too angry. I start thinking about the last essay Mrs. Barton assigned, *What would Be Difficult to Give Up?*

I take out my notebook and a pencil.

Where is Bri?

CHAPTER 17

Action Scene
Einstein and Cookies

Sam

On the bus ride in, I notice the shrine is growing. There is more everything. I wonder if she saw it coming. I wonder if she was scared. I wonder about her kids. Then I feel sick and need to stop.

Where is Bri? I'm looking in all the locker sections for her. Not in ours, not in Jay's, not in Mandy's. Meg asks what my mania is all about.

"I have to tell Bri to hide her book," I say.

Meg is looking at me weird. I realize she thinks there are many things wrong with this sentence. I can't even begin to explain.

When I, finally, get to lunch, I'm still searching for Bri. I don't want her to show up in English without warning of new lady's dumbness. But I don't see her anywhere.

Rachel and Zack are holding hands. Jay's spinning a basketball on his finger. Mandy is touching up her makeup. Life goes on for them. Nothing has changed for them. This is the first time I've ever looked at the herd with envy.

Miss Lee asks for my book the second I get to class. I tell her it's at home, and I'll bring it tomorrow. This is a lie. It's in my backpack. I wonder if she can feel its presence in the room, and it is calling out "ha, ha" to her. This lie also buys me two more days. I won't be here tomorrow. I'm going to the funeral.

Miss Lee passes out noun worksheets and tells us to complete them in class. She says we have to work in *silence*. How can I possibly work in silence with this screaming inside my head? Why can't we ever work in noise? Why can't we work as loud as we want while she's quiet? I intend to clear my throat a lot and turn my pages with abandon.

The entire first sheet is making nouns plural. I admit, there was some challenge attached to this in first grade, but now, come on. As I'm laughing at our work, she starts packing up Mrs. Barton's desk. She pulls things out of draws and shoves them in boxes. She clears everything off the top, even the mug Mrs. Barton's kids made for her. She shouldn't be touching that stuff. I feel like flinging erasers again, but instead, I ask, "Miss Lee, how do you make century plural?"

She tells me to just add an s. Thanks, Einstein. Centurys. Mike cracks up, and this is enough for me. I decide to "just add an s" to every word on the page. This is way more fun than thinking. Some of my favorite new words are babys, ladys, crys, trys, and storys. I love following directions.

Miss Lee has the desk all boxed up. She starts ripping down the bulletin board. She tears down and throws away all our color essays.

Using this Miss Lee-method, I'm able to finish my work quickly and have time to start my own project.

What Annoys Me Most About Miss Lee
Sam Cooper

Miss Lee is the most annoying person I have ever met in my entire life. How can I begin to list the many, many annoying things about her?

I'd like to start with the obvious. Miss Lee is here. The fact that she is in this room annoys me. She shouldn't be here. Mrs. Barton should be. But if Miss Lee has to be here, does she need to wear that ugly pink jumper with the fuchsia turtleneck? I didn't know they made those in grown-up sizes. It makes me flashback to nursery school where kids cried at drop off and wiped snot on the tables. There should, at least, be smocks.

There's also the fact that she is completely destroying the room. Did she think it would be a comfort to us if she removed every single memory of Mrs. Barton? Does she think that if she boxes everything away, we will forget Mrs. Barton ever existed and stop being sad? Her parents definitely made her rip Band-Aids off fast. Jerks, that ruins lives.

There is also this *minor* detail. She is not teaching us what Mrs. Barton wanted us to learn. She's giving us busy work so we will shut up so she can rip apart more memories. We are supposed to be finishing this book so we know what Mrs. Barton wanted us to learn. We are supposed to be writing essays to figure out things we didn't know about our world and ourselves.

Maybe she'll introduce story time and snack. I like snack.

I see Mandy and Jay on my way out of the building. Aren't they even the slightest bit concerned that Bri is missing? Why are they laughing? I freak out.

"Hey, idiots!" I scream. "Where's Bri?"

Mandy is making a face at me, and Jay says he hasn't heard from her in a while.

"Are you morons kidding me? What kind of friends are you? She's been absent for two days. Did it occur to either of you to check on her?" I'm screaming.

I'm too mad to get on the bus. I start walking away. I don't know where I'm going. It's my new thing.

I decide to check out this shrine. I'm still hoping it can make me feel better. I call my mom and ask her if she can pick me up there. I head down the sidewalk after the buses go by. People have left all kinds of things here. I wonder if I came here with flowers if I'd think about what color or kind she liked. I don't know, so I wouldn't pick flowers. I don't get the stuffed animals. She doesn't seem the type who'd want those. I think that I'd like to leave my copy of *When I Grew Up*, but she'd never forgive me if I ruined a book by leaving in out in the rain. I don't think I'd be able to forgive myself either.

This isn't a happy place. I don't like it here. This doesn't make me feel better. There's still a bunch of glass in the road. Putting stuff on top of it doesn't make it go away.

My mom is coming up the street now. I get ready to get in the car when I hear a buzzing from the pile of stuff. I see Bri's phone. I pick it up and see "Missed Call Jay" and "Missed Call Dad."

"Mom, we have to go to Bri's now," I'm almost yelling.

Bri, with no phone, is like me with no sarcasm. This is a problem.

We get to the house. I am simultaneously banging on the door and ringing the bell. Then I add screaming her name to the cadence. I think about kicking in the door like they do in movies. That would be a lot of fun to try. I wonder if I'd break my foot. I wonder if it's really possible, or if it's just one of those things that happens in movies that can never happen in life. Stop it! Stop thinking about action films! Focus!

Bri opens the door a crack. She looks awful. I haven't seen her without makeup in three years. She's wearing gray sweats and a white T-shirt. Her hair is pulled back in a messy bun.

"What?"

"I wanted to see if you were alive? Are you alive? I can't tell," I say.

"Is there a reason why you are here?" Bri asks in a daze.

"I found your phone, and there's all this stuff going on and—" she cuts me off and screams at me to go away. She means it so I do not attempt to kick in her door, but instead, I just go home.

Bri's a zombie. Bri's not supposed to be a zombie. I need Bri to not be a zombie. Is there a book around here with a cure for zombies?

Too much is happening.

I ask my mom for some help in the kitchen. About an hour later, she drives me back to Bri's.

I ring the doorbell once and wait. This way she won't think it's me.

"What part of go away and leave me alone do you not understand?" Bri yells.

"But I made cookies," I say.

Bri just starts laughing. The whole scene is so crazy that she has to laugh. Sam made cookies and brought them over?

"Really? Cookies?" Bri asks. "When is the funeral?"

"We'll be here at eleven," I say.

"Okay, and Sam, thanks."

CHAPTER 18

Church
Last Parade

Sam

I hate this. I don't know what to expect. My mom says I was at my grandmother's funeral. I don't remember it. I pull on the clothes Mom set out for me and finish getting ready.

When we get to Bri's, she's waiting outside. It's freezing. She looks like she's been out there awhile. She said her mom was asleep and didn't want to take any chances on how I was going to alert her to my presence on the front stoop, so she thought she'd just wait outside. No one speaks on the way.

When we get close to the church, I can see a mob gathered outside. There are more than I can count. My mom drives around awhile to find a place to park. She finally settles on a spot around the block. Then we walk in silence to join the mob. Everyone is filing in to the church now. We go in and sit.

The crowd has a lot of kids in it. Students, I guess. There are little kids too. I can't look at them too long.

Bagpipes can now be heard. They are the sound of misery. The music grows louder as they come in to the church. We all stand and watch the procession coming in. It looks like a sad parade. After the bagpipers, there is a casket draped in white flowers. Then her family comes down the aisle. There's a man carrying a little boy who's got his head buried in the man's neck. His other arm holds the hand of another boy, a bit older, who's just staring in front of him. The man looks so tired. I think about how he's probably walked with his boys like this before, but it was on his way to the monorail after a long day in Disney World. I guess these are her husband and children. I don't know how they can stand up there. How are they going through these motions?

I've had a steady stream of tears running down my cheeks since the music started, but when I see her boys, I start sobbing and shaking. I'm crying so hard, my lungs hurt. I force myself to pretend it's not real, just so I can get myself together. I pretend it's a movie. I pretend it's a joke. I pretend there's not a coffin but a girl in a white gown coming down the aisle. You don't have to pick what side you're on at a funeral.

We take our seats again. I cannot take my eyes off the boys. When I can't take looking at them anymore, I stare at the coffin. Then I can't take looking at that anymore, so I look back at the boys. This is such a mess. Mrs. Barton didn't want this. It's not fair.

The reverend has begun speaking about her. He says she was a devoted daughter, sister, wife, mother, and teacher. Those are a lot of things to be. You don't think of all the other things someone is, just the part they are to you. He tells a story about how she always wanted to become a teacher that even as a young girl, she knew she was going to help other people see how much they mattered to the world. She was going to help them see that their story was important.

I can't breathe when he says this. I look away, down, over, out, anywhere to put me back in the movie and out of this reality. He finishes by saying he would like to welcome anyone who would like to speak to come up to the lectern. I get up automatically and get behind the microphone.

"Mrs. Barton told us we should write something when we have something to say. I have something to say." I pull the essay I wrote in the bathroom out of my pocket.

"On our last day together, Mrs. Barton assigned the essay *What would Be Difficult to Give Up*. Mrs. Barton gave us a lot of chances to write. She thought if we could write things down, we would be better communicators. She had this really simple idea that if we could express ourselves and listen to each other, the world, or at least middle school, could be easier to get through. It seemed like a lot of the other kids in my class got this right away, but not me. I mean, it's hard to open up like that and expect anything descent to happen in return. But I knew Mrs. Barton would help me. Now, she can't, and I'm not really sure what to do about that because the thing that would be most difficult to give up is her."

I go back to my seat. Bri tries to say something to me. I can't hear her.

"Go to school tomorrow, Bri," I say. "We've got work to do."

Bri

I can't believe that Sam came over twice. I can't believe she made cookies. It's so crazy. She is picking me up for the funeral, which I really appreciate because I did not know how I was going to get there.

I am a little nervous. I have never been to a funeral, and I really don't know what to expect. Sam was coming at 11:00 a.m., but I was ready at 10:00 a.m. I sat on a chair in the living room and just waited for her to come. Everything that has happened kept going around in my head. Everything from when Sam and I were friends to the beginning of the school year to Mrs. Barton. I still could not believe that she is gone. Just like that.

I decide that I should wait outside. My mother is sleeping, and I know I can't deal with her now. At exactly 11:00 a.m., Mrs. Cooper and Sam got to my house.

It was a pretty quiet drive. Everybody seemed to be lost in her own thoughts. I felt sorry for Mrs. Cooper. She just looked so worried about us but knows there is nothing she can say.

When we pulled up to the church, the first thing I noticed was how many people were there. There were people everywhere. There were people actually waiting to get inside. Sam's mom couldn't find anywhere to park, so eventually, she just parked down the block.

We are greeted by the sad sound of bagpipes. It's almost as if the entire church itself is weeping. Mixed together with this is the sound of sobbing. It is truly a sad symphony. The air is filled with the smell of carnations.

We stand and watch the casket, draped with flowers, come down the aisle with her family behind her. Her husband looks like he is exhausted, but he has to hold it together because he is carrying one of the little boys and holding the other one's hand. I recognize the little boys from the picture on Mrs. Barton's desk. I can tell they are the same boys, but they look really different. These children will never be the same again. These little boys lost their mommy, and they will never be the same again. It is this thought that just makes me lose it.

Sam must be thinking something along those lines because she is sobbing too. We take our seats, and the reverend starts to talk about her, about her life. Not just her teacher life, her real life, where she was a wife, a mother, a daughter, and a sister. It's weird how I always think of her as Mrs. Barton, the teacher.

She has a first name. Of course, she has a first name. Duh. I just never thought of her as Faith Barton. I never thought of her as Faith, or as Mommy. This brings on a whole new batch of tears. If I am this upset that I lost my teacher, how bad must her family feel? This thought does little to comfort me. In fact, it makes me cry more. The reverend talks more about how Mrs. Barton always wanted to be a teacher. He asks if anyone would like to say something about Mrs. Barton, and surprisingly, Sam gets up.

Sam talks about how Mrs. Barton was such a great teacher that inspired us all. Then she reads the most beautiful essay about Mrs. Barton being the most difficult thing to give up. It is just so beautiful. I feel exactly the same way. When she comes back to the seat, I lean over and whisper to her that Mrs. Barton would be proud of her for sharing her story.

I don't think she heard me. She tells me to go to school tomorrow. She says we have work to do.

I have to go to school tomorrow because Sam wants me to. And Mrs. Barton would want me to.

CHAPTER 19

Back to School
Hide Your Book and Release the Kraken

Sam and Bri

The ride home from the funeral, yesterday, was quiet, but I did manage to tell Bri I wanted to let her in on some things before she showed up in English. I went straight to her locker in the morning and told her we needed to talk at lunch.

"And don't forget to hide your book," I call back to her. I forget to explain to her that I've become a crazy person and am insanely obsessed with not turning in *When I Grew Up*. I wouldn't give this book back to Miss Lee if my life depended on it. Actually, right now, my life depends on keeping it.

When I get to lunch, I see Bri is waiting. I tell Meg I have to talk to her. As Meg looks at me with continued confusion, I realize I have not yet explained anything that's been going on to her. Note to self, have conversation with Meg soon so she doesn't have me committed. I go to sit across from her and start telling her everything about stupid Miss Lee and her reign of terror. I begin listing compelling evidence.

"She packed up the desk and threw out our favorite color essays," I say.

"Maybe someone asked her to pack things up?" Bri offers.

"What about throwing the essays away? We were all right in front of her. She could have asked. And she wears jumpers. Jumpers! People don't wear jumpers," I say.

"Wearing a jumper doesn't make you evil. You wear bad clothes all the time, and you're not really evil," jokes Bri.

"What about puppies?" I say.

"What do you mean, 'What about puppies?'" Bri says.

"She thinks the plural is p-u-p-p-y-s. She hates dogs," I say.

"Bad spelling doesn't make you *bad*. When did you go crazy?" Bri asks.

"I went crazy when this idiot entered my world. She's ruining the only thing of Mrs. Barton that we have left. She's not collecting our group project. She doesn't want our essays. She said out loud that she wants us to *forget* how class used to be," I say.

"Sam, it sounds like you are overreacting. I'm sure she's not that bad. You just don't like her because she is not Mrs. Barton. I get that, but she can't be that bad," Bri tries to reason.

"You think I'm overreacting. Wait until you see the room. Wait until she starts talking. She's ridiculous, Bri," Sam says.

We get up to class. Miss Lee tells us to wait in the back until she "places" us. She puts us in new seats, boy/girl. This is cute. I feel so fair and balanced. I also feel like I am now better able to focus on Miss Lee's offerings of wisdom now that I am surrounded by boys. Boys are not at all distracting. That Miss Lee is just filled with great ideas. She must have been up all night thinking of this. I stare at Bri to confirm she is acknowledging the dumbness.

Right on cue, Miss Lee asks me for my book. I tell her I forgot it. She asks Bri for her copy too. Bri says she'll bring it tomorrow. Miss Lee informs us that she will write us up if we show up without it. Thank you, Miss Lee. Sounds like a plan.

Next order of stupid business. Miss Lee passes out a list of class rules. "No gum, no pens, no frayed edges, and absolutely, no *paper clips*. Any multiple-page assignment is to be stapled *only*. Paper clips are unnecessary objects. I don't want to see them."

Thank you, Miss Lee, for the new rules, without which, I would be unable to keep myself in line.

I decide to compliment her on her blue jumper and ask her a follow-up question on plural nouns. Today's word, business. Will she suggest b-u-s-i-n-e-s-s-s?

This really is one of my favorite new games.

I decide, again, to pursue my own endeavors.

Things I could do to annoy Miss Lee:

1. activate stink bomb
    a. obtain bomb
    b. secure nasal passageway obstructers in order to not smell stink
    c. rig detonation device
2. plant whoopee cushion on seat
    a. obtain whoopee cushion
    b. sneak into room
    c. enjoy horrified look of Miss Lee wondering if she's soiled her jumper
3. release kraken
    a. obtain kraken
    b. fashion toga out of sheet
    c. release kraken while in secure location
4. ding-dong ditch
    a. find out where Miss Lee lives
    b. find out if she has doorbell
    c. ring and run

Maybe I could try a good old-fashioned book drop. I look up at the clock and select exactly 1:45 p.m. I need to wait three minutes and thirteen seconds. I get my math book ready on the corner of my desk and wait. Finally, it's time! My book lands on the floor with a thud. I'm staring at Miss Lee to watch her reaction. She asks me why I'm staring at her and tells me she thinks I've dropped my book.

Things to do before I annoy Miss Lee:

1. consider number of participants as factor; and
2. research effectiveness of lone protests.

"What did she say?" Sam says.

"She said we need to write a convictive essay about why the school year should be longer than 180 days," Bri says.

"What does convictive mean?" Sam asks.

"I don't know. Ask her."

"Um, excuse me, Miss Lee, what does convictive mean?"

"Intelligent children should know what it means. I believe *you* should know what it means, and if you do not, perhaps you should look it up in a dictionary," Miss Lee snaps.

"Jeez," Sam says, "I just asked."

With that, Sam gets up, gets a dictionary, and stands in the back of the room looking it up. Then Bri gets up, and she gets a dictionary. Then Joe Ryan and Marc Jones get up and get dictionaries. Then Kaitlyn and Stacy get up, until the whole class, including Michael, is standing in the back of the room looking in dictionaries.

It is evident that this entire situation really flusters Miss Lee. She looks like she is going to explode.

"I am ordering you to sit down. All you!" she screeches. "This is not acceptable behavior! Sit down!"

We all make our way back to our seats, laughing. This must be some kind of joke because who yells like that over something so trivial?

"Calm down, lady," Joe mumbles.

After everyone is back in their seats, Miss Lee tries to regain her composure. "Can anyone tell us what convictive means?"

Bri raises her hand and says, "It means persuasive."

Sam mumbles, "Why couldn't you just say persuasive?"

"Yes, that is correct, young lady," Miss Lee says to Bri.

Sam raises her hand. Miss Lee sighs heavily and says, "Yes?"

"If this is a persuasive composition, can I take the opposing side of the issue?" Sam asks.

"No, absolutely not. Everyone must write a thousand-word essay about why we should be in school more than 180 days," Miss Lee responds.

The entire class moaned as the bell rang.

"Okay, class dismissed."

As everyone was filing out of the room, Bri walks tentatively up to Miss Lee.

"Hi, Miss Lee. My name is Brianna Drew. Everybody calls me Bri. I know you are new, but this really isn't how things work around here. Persuasive compositions are supposed to be shorter than one thousand words, and well, we should get to pick our own side of the issue."

"Brianna, thanks for your advice, but if I need your help, I'll ask for it. Good day," Miss Lee answered.

"Okay, I was just trying to help," Bri says. "See ya."

Bri quickly grabbed her stuff and ran out the door.

Sam was waiting for her.

"Well," Sam asks, "was I exaggerating?"

"No, you're right. She's a witch. So what do we do about it?"

Time to launch the paper clip revolution.

CHAPTER 20

Sam's House
Launching the Plan

Sam and Bri

"Okay, Sam, we really need to talk. Miss Lee has some serious issues," Bri says.

"We need to send her a message that we are not okay with the way she is doing things," Sam says.

"What can we do? Is she insane? What is her problem with paper clips? Does anyone use them for assignments anyway?" Bri asks.

"Maybe she's afraid they will get stuck on her jumper," Sam jokes. "We need to get together to plan our paper clip revolution. I'll come to your house?"

"Um, let's go to your house. I think we'll need cookies for this." Bri chuckles.

Later at Sam's, Bri and Sam are discussing Mrs. Barton and the lessons that she taught them.

"Sam, Mrs. Barton really wanted us to read *When I Grew Up*. It was her favorite book. There must be a reason why she loved it so much," Bri says.

"Everything she did was for a reason. We have to figure it out," Sam says.

"Do you really think Miss Lee is that stupid, or do you think she's just clueless?" Bri asks.

"I think she's sent here by an alien race to destroy children's hopes and dreams, one English class at a time," Sam says.

"Well, I agree that we need to send her a message," Bri confers. "I got it! What if we don't write the essay she assigned but instead, write a different essay?"

Sam says, "Can we at least explore the option of kraken release?"

Bri's not listening.

"Then we get everyone else to write the same essay! It's perfect!" Bri exclaims.

"Can you get everyone to go along with you?" Sam says.

"Of course. All I have to do is post it on Facebook, tweet, and text, and it's done." Bri laughs. "Don't forget, everybody *loves* me."

"They love you like Lee loves paper clips," Sam says.

"I have the perfect topic! Why it is important for children to express themselves," Bri suggests.

"I'm writing about how suppressing a child's right to self-expression leads to daydreaming about kraken release," Sam says. "Okay, that's part one of operation paper clip, but we need something else."

"I still think we need to finish the book," Bri says.

"So we finish it. What if the whole class leaves, just walks out, and goes somewhere to read and discuss the book?" Sam says.

"We only have our two copies. She collected the rest," Bri says.

"Okay, I'll get Jack to get them," Sam says.

"What does Jack have to do with us getting the books?"

"Jack is trained in special ops. He'll find a way," Sam says.

"That would certainly send a message," Bri agrees. "Do you think everyone will leave class?"

"You're the popular one. Take care of it," Sam says.

"Let's do it. Mrs. Barton would want us to," Bri says.

Bri got to work. She posted on Facebook, "Hey, eighth-period English—Miss Lee's class. We are looking for soldiers for operation paper clip. We are taking back our class with a two-part plan."

"Step one. New essay. Why it is important for children to express themselves. *You must use paper clips on your paper! The more the better!*"

"Step two. Everyone walks in class, drops essay on Lee's desk, and then leaves class. *We will conduct our own class outside.*"

Bri also sends out a mass text to everyone.

Sam stands over her shoulder. "You're an evil genius. I never knew that about you." She laughs.

"Thanks, I try," Bri laughs. "Seriously, I don't think Miss Lee is evil. Maybe she just doesn't know any better. Maybe she can't see our side."

"Yeah, maybe, or maybe she's just stupid," Sam adds.

CHAPTER 21

School
The Paper Clip Revolution

Sam and Bri

Sam walked up to Bri's locker. Today was the day that they would take their class back.

"Are we ready?" Sam asks.

"Yup. Do you have your essay?"

"Duh. I used ten paper clips. They're all different colors too. Do you think that'll make a statement?" Sam says.

"I think it will. Is there any significance to the colors?" Bri asks.

"Each represents a memory of all my special time with you. Shut up!" Sam says.

Michael Delnick comes up to the girls in the hallway. He looks a little nervous.

"Hey, guys. I just wanted to tell you I'm glad you are doing what you're doing. She needs to be stopped. We need to get our class back."

"Thanks, Michael," says Bri.

"Thanks, Dork," says Sam.

"See you later, Sam."

"Bri, you know something?"

"What?"

"You're not half as bad as you used to be."

"Gee, thanks, I think."

Finally, when it feels like it will never get here, it is eighth period. Everyone walks into class one at a time, like a beautiful synchronized dance. Each student goes up to Miss Lee's desk, puts his or her paper down, and walks out the door.

At first, she doesn't know how to react. She looks truly shocked. Then she seems to panic. When the panic starts, so does the yelling.

"Get back here right now! All of you! This is not acceptable!" she screamed.

Bri and Sam lead the entire class down the hall and out the front door of the building. Since it was such a warm day, they think it would be a good idea to have class outside. Once everyone is out there, Bri addresses the class.

"Thank you, everyone, for supporting this. We really think Mrs. Barton would want us to finish this book." Bri points to Sam holding her copy of *When I Grew Up*. "She felt this was important, so we need to find out why. We owe it to her."

All the students sat down in a large circle in the warm sun. It is just so soothing to be in the sun after such a long hard winter, such long hard days. Just as the students began to read the book, Sam looks up to see Miss Lee looking out the window watching them, and Sam thinks she sees her reading their essays.

Mr. Riley was, of course, called when the class left. He immediately ran outside to see these "unruly" students having an English class. He just stands off to the side watching, amazed that the class is being led by two students.

He waits in the distance until they finished. Then Mr. Riley goes over to speak to them.

"Ladies, I didn't know what to think at first, but I'm proud of what you've done here. Mrs. Barton taught you well. But we can't hold every class out here, and you've got a teacher upstairs that may need a second chance."

"A second chance? Do you know she won't even let us finish the book we are in the middle of reading? She's crazy!" Bri yells.

Sam quietly grabs Bri's arm and says, "Bri, look."

They look up and see Miss Lee still watching out the window. They wonder if she was able to hear. They tell Mr. Riley they will stay in class tomorrow and give it a try.

Sam

I don't know what it was, but I just didn't feel like being angry anymore. Maybe it was seeing Miss Lee looking pitiful as she stared out the window. Maybe it was reading the book together, like we knew we were supposed to. Maybe it was just that as Mrs. Barton's student, I should know better. I just felt like we all got ripped apart enough. I can't be in any more pieces. Being out there together, reading, it felt like Mrs. Barton was right there, too, asking us to remember what she was trying to teach us.

CHAPTER 22

Why Children Need to Express Themselves Essays Post-War Wound Licking

Sam and Bri

The next day, we go to class just like we promised Mr. Riley we would. Miss Lee is leaning on the front of the desk. She's usually seated behind it. She looks more like a person like this, like she's not scared of us. There might even be half a smile there. She lets us sit down and settle ourselves instead of screaming at us to do what we are already doing. This is, also, a nice change.

"Bri, would you mind if I read your essay?" she asks.

Wow, she's acknowledging what we wrote.

"Sure, I don't mind," replies Bri.

"Why it is important for children to express themselves? A blank canvass. Unshaped clay. A barren landscape. These are all words that describe our young minds. Children need to be given the opportunity to express themselves so they can become themselves. Take the blank canvass for example. If children have the opportunity to paint with colors of their choice, their world can grow. Who's to say, which shade of blue should be used on a sky, or even if the sky should be blue at all? From when children are very small, they are told what colors to use, and they are told to color in the lines. Why? I say everyone should color, or paint something whatever color they see it. If you feel a woman should have purple hair, give her purple hair. Why do we need to stay in the lines?" Furthermore, the unshaped clay literally describes our minds. That clay, in the hands with the right pressure and finesse, can turn into something beautiful. It can be molded into anything. If students are given a chance to do this, to mold the clay and think for themselves, amazing things will happen. Teachers not only have to be aware of this but also allow this to happen and encourage it. They need to foster it. If teachers don't mold this clay, they may as well let it harden into a clump. If students are allowed and encouraged to express themselves, they will flourish. Some will grow into roses, others tomato plants, and some, mighty oaks with strong roots. It doesn't matter what as long as they are allowed to grow and express themselves. When students are given ridiculous, strict guidelines and boundaries, it's just like pouring weed killer on your garden. We are not weeds. "Sam, can I read yours?" Miss Lee asks.

I have to admit, my first instinct is to say no because I'm so used to not trusting her, but something feels different. I look over at Bri. She mouths, "It's okay."

"Yeah, go ahead," I say.

"Why it is important for children to express themselves? Children first learn to express themselves in order to prevent peeing their pants. Children value this expression because they need help and are trying to avoid being wet and cold. Parents value this because, come on, let's face it, no one wants to clean that crud up. Expression is good. Children also need to express themselves so they can tell people what they think is important. Everyone needs to be heard and made to feel like what they say matters. If you cork up this expression, children will explode. Exploding is bad. I would like to name some examples of people who had their expressive flows blocked: the devil, Hitler, the Delightful Children from *Codename: Kids Next Door*, and Plankton. These people all turned to evildoing because no one ever let them express how they felt. Evil is bad.

86

There are things I might do if left to feel stifled. I might research employing mythical creatures to do my biding. I might get my wand and practice the Unforgivable Curses. I might go to Walmart and poke holes in the birdseed bags. I might short sheet my family's beds. I might even go shoe shopping. Shopping is bad. Therefore, in order to prevent the threat of my wetting myself, exploding, turning evil, or shopping, I beg you to *let me express myself!*"

Then Miss Lee told us all we could have hoped for.

"We have had a very difficult beginning. I don't suppose we could have met under any worse of a circumstance. Mrs. Barton was important to you all. I always understood that, but I wasn't very good about letting you know how sad I felt for your loss and how challenged I felt about taking her place. I always knew hers were big shoes to fill. I want to tell all of you, I'm sorry. I'm sorry you lost this amazing person. I'm sorry I can't be her. I'd like to start over. Why don't you tell me about her?"

CHAPTER 23

School
Mrs. Barton's Room

Sam

It's been a few weeks since The Paperclip Revolution. Miss Lee has actually been pretty cool. She can't hear the books talk in the library or anything, but she learned how to listen to us. We learned how to hear her too.

Now that the weather has broken, we can go ahead with the tree-planting ceremony. Miss Lee suggested the idea. We are going to plant it out in the front of the building where we had our first paper clip meeting.

A bunch of us got together to figure out what the plaque should say. We decided on "In Loving Memory of Faith Barton and Her Continuing Story."

Donations came in from students, parents, and faculty to help us buy the benches and tables. It's the first outside classroom our school has ever had. We call it Mrs. Barton's room. She would have loved this.

A few days after the ceremony, we went out to Mrs. Barton's room to finish *When I Grew Up*. It turned out to be pretty easy to guess why it was one of her favorite books. The book is about seeing different sides of the same story. Mrs. Barton loved that stuff.

It's about the whole idea that we can be on different sides and that's okay as long as we respect each other's views. And we have to be brave enough to say how we feel. Mrs. Barton made us courageous.

Every day, I go out into this same crazy world, but it doesn't seem as bad. I guess I've changed. I shouldn't be waiting until I'm old enough to vote to participate in life. There are things to care about now, right here in front of me. And when the stupid comes around, as it always goes, Mrs. Barton taught me how to get through it. I listen to the person's side and then share mine. Sometimes you meet in the middle of the differences. Sometimes you realize there is no difference at all. And sometimes you discover there are even more things to discuss.

I like feeling like people can learn something from me. It's even easier to have conversations with people when you give them the benefit of the doubt. Like when I suggested the pet-adoption day to student council for the second time. I didn't talk to them like they were idiots. I spoke to them like they were people. I explained why I thought it was important, heard their concerns, and we worked it all out. It's been a lot of fun getting ready for adoption day. Yeah, I said it, fun. Seeing Jack, Jay, Mandy, and Meg all come together, well, it's like the paper clip revolution just keeps going.

CHAPTER 24

School on Saturday
Sam Smiles

Bri

I cannot believe that it is a Saturday, and I am getting up early to work at the Adopt-a-Pet Day at the shelter. And that's not the only shocker. I am actually looking forward to it. When Sam first mentioned this a few months ago, I was like, are you kidding me? And now, I'm actually looking forward to this day.

It seems that a lot has changed, but then I think it's more like things changed back to the way they used to be. It's almost like there was a strange switch that was flipped. After The Paperclip Revolution, as it is known throughout the school, things were just different.

First, there was Mr. Riley telling Sam and me how proud he was of us. Then there was Miss Lee actually apologizing to us. She has gotten so much better. Her class is actually fun. She isn't Mrs. Barton, but then again, nobody can ever be her. But that doesn't mean she doesn't have something to teach us, or that she doesn't have a story to tell us.

See, I think I get what Mrs. Barton was trying to get into our thick heads. She wanted us to know, to understand, that people see things differently. Everyone thinks her way is the right way, that her side is the right side. Everyone thinks her story is the most important. The trick is to listen to someone else's side and then tell your side. If people listen to each other's stories, they can learn a lot. This is *huge*! Why don't more people know this?

And then, perhaps the most miraculous of the changes is Madame Miserable is not miserable anymore. I can no longer call her that. Now she's just Sarcastic Sam. She is so different. She's, dare I say, happy! As I said, she's still sarcastic, but that's her, and truly, I wouldn't want her any other way. But she's not mean anymore. She's more thoughtful now. She's more considerate now.

When she presented her idea for the pet adoption day the second time. She actually presented it instead of demanding it and treating us all like her stupid minions. We had to go along with her because she made such a great case for the animals, yes, but also because she put herself out there and actually *asked* us for help. It was so much fun to work together for a change. It felt like we were in elementary school again. It's nice to have Sam in my life again. It's nice to have her on my side.

"Hey, Bri," Sam shouts, "that family over there wants to adopt! Patch has a home!"

I chuckle as I say, "That's great, Sam."

She looks like Christmas morning grinning ear to ear.

CHAPTER 25

Soccer Field
Bugs and BBQ Chips

Sam and Bri

"No," Sam says.

"Why?" Bri says.

"Because it's dumb," Sam replies.

"Please. I came to adoption day," Bri pleads.

"No," Sam says.

"Sam, come on," Bri says.

"Fine. I'll go to the stupid game," Sam says in surrender.

"Yay, I'm so happy. It'll be so much fun!" Bri says.

"For you," Sam replies.

It's hot, and there are bugs, but Sam shows up to the dumb Girls' County Championship Soccer Game.

"Yay, you're here!" Bri says.

"Duh, I told you I'd be here," Sam says.

"I saved you a seat right there in front. And I brought you water and a snack because I know you'll get cranky without it," Bri says.

"I'm not five," Sam says.

"Yes, you are," Bri replies.

Sam

She saved me a seat midfield, right in front. From here, it will be impossible to feign attention. I'll be forced to see every play and hear every cheer. And have I mentioned the heat and bugs? This is cruel and unusual punishment.

The players have taken the field to warm up. Just then, Jay, Jack, Rachel, and Zach come over to say hi to Bri and take their seats on either side of me.

"I didn't know Bri would want witnesses to record every detail of my pain," Sam says.

Jack and Jay laugh. Jack says, "Wait."

"Yeah, wait. It gets better," Jay adds.

"I'm glad everything is all Kumbaya now, but I need some time to adjust to you two finishing each other's sentences," Sam says.

Bri, Mandy, and the other loud girls start cheering. There is a lot of noise, kicking, jumping, and clapping, but look at Bri. She looks so happy. It's kinda like her thing—spreading happy. It's as if she's in this world to make sure the happy doesn't run out. She makes sure it's right there in front of you in case you need any.

The players come to the sideline now. Jack nudges me hard in the ribs and points to number fifteen.

"No way! Is that…did you guys know?" Sam says.

They are all cracking up. Bri is watching me too. Number fifteen turns to look at me and shrugs.

It occurs to me I never asked Meg what she was doing when she couldn't hang out. Okay, Meg plays soccer. You can really miss stuff when you're not paying attention.

Bri is jumping around like a freak now.

"Sam, look, Meg has a story," Bri says.

"Yeah, funny. Stop being mental," Sam says.

The players take the field, and Meg is still great. She was better than everyone when we were little, too, and she always loved it. I'm glad she didn't give it up. I just feel bad she didn't tell me. But when did I give her the chance to? I was always talking, complaining. She probably thought I'd make fun of her. And she would have been right. That's not me anymore. I'm going to have to ask her all about it.

I stand up and scream as loud as I can, "Let's go, Meg!" I even let out a hoot and a holler.

The crowd is in a frenzy now, on its feet clapping and cheering. I look over at Bri, and she's pointing at me. She smiles and claps for me.

With Meg's help, our team kicked their butts and won county finals. Meg was voted MVP. I can't believe I could have missed this.

After the game, I tell Bri, "Thanks, and next time, don't pack me BBQ chips. I like sour cream and onion better." Then I find Meg to tell her how great she did.

CHAPTER 26

Dress Shopping
Everyone Likes Not to Look
Stupid for Future Generations

Sam and Bri

The end of the year is coming on fast now. Finals are this week. Bri and Sam decide to study for English together.

"I hate finals week. Why do we have to have finals? Why do we have to take a test on things we've already taken tests on? It's like showering after showering. This is so stupid," Sam says.

"No one likes finals. At least tomorrow's the last day. How are we supposed to remember all the way back to September?" Bri says.

"September was a lifetime ago. Things were different," Sam says.

"Yeah, you used to be a big jerk," Bri says.

"I know. What was wrong with me? I was so mad at everybody for not being as smart as I am," Sam says.

"Remember I said 'used to be,'" Bri says.

"That came out wrong. I mean, I thought everyone was stupid. I wasn't giving anyone the chance to prove me wrong. But you weren't so great yourself," Sam says.

"There was nothing wrong with how I was acting in September. I'm always nice to everybody," Bri says.

"What about me?" Sam asks.

"You were the exception. A lot has happened this year," Bri says.

"You had a really cool skirt on the first day," Sam says.

"What? You remember my skirt," Bri says.

"I think skirts are stupid, but I can still see them," Sam says.

"I know you saw the skirt, but you remember the skirt? Wow, there are so many layers to you," Bri says.

"You always remember what I wear," Sam says.

"It's not too hard to remember your signature black shirt and black pants. It's kind of like your uniform," Bri jokes. "Can your mom still take us dress shopping tomorrow after finals? Mandy and Meg want to come."

"I wish I wanted to come. I don't see what the big deal is. I was going to wear my Flash costume, but yeah, my mom can take us," Sam says.

"You should want to come because you should care what you look like. Someday your kids will see a picture of you from your eighth-grade dance. Do you want them to see you looking like a freak?" Bri asks.

"Why would I bring children into this overpopulated world?" Sam replies.

"See you tomorrow," Bri says.

After finals, Sam's mom picked up the girls and took them to some dress shops.

"Hey, Bri," Sam says, "look at this! This is perfect for you!" Sam holds up a gold sequined dress. "It will make you look like a princess."

"I've never seen a princess wear gold sequins. That looks like something Lady Gaga would wear." Bri laughs. "Wait here. You have to try this on, Sam. This is perfect for you." Bri hands Sam a black dress. "Trust me."

Sam goes to the dressing room and comes out a minute later. The second she comes out, the three girls and Mrs. Cooper start laughing hysterically. Sam comes walking out wearing a bright-pink Southern belle dress with a giant hoop slip underneath it.

"I call this look Southern hell," Sam says in her best Southern accent.

"Wow. That's even too pink for me!" Bri quips. "Hey! Is that your coming-out dress? Do you want to go to a debutante ball? You're all ready for it! Presenting the one and only Miss Samantha Cooper."

"Please stare at me! I am on display! As you judge my physical appearance, please know I am dreaming that an opportunity will arise soon for me to show you I know what all the forks at the table are for," Sam says.

Sam then curtsies. Everyone is laughing so hard.

"Where did you get that, Sam?" her mom asks.

"Someone left it back there in the reject pile," Sam says.

"Ha, ha. Now, will you please go try on the black dress," Bri says.

"Okay, okay."

A couple of minutes later, Sam comes out wearing the black dress.

"You look so pretty," Mandy says.

"It's perfect," says Meg.

"You look like a girl! I can't believe it! Underneath the uniform, you are a girl!" Bri jokes.

"My little girl is all grown-up," Mrs. Cooper joins in on the fun.

"*Aw*, come on. This is dumb," Sam says. "Everyone likes to not look stupid, including me. Do I look stupid?"

All at once they all reply, "*No!*"

"Sam, I was teasing you. You look awesome," Bri says.

"I feel stupid," Sam says.

"You need to get used to it," Bri says.

"Why?" Sam asks.

"Because when you run for Congress, you need to be dressed like a person," Bri says.

A few minutes later, Bri comes out in her pale-pink dress.

Everyone was just looking at her, not saying anything.

Bri turned to Sam. "Okay, let's hear it, Sam. What do you got? Do I look like I stole Miss Piggy's pretty pink dress? Does it look like I spilled Pepto on me? Come on, the suspense is killing me!" Bri says.

"I'm trying, but I got nothing. You look great. It's perfect," Sam says.

"What? Who are you, and what have you done with Sam? First, a pretty dress, and now, no sarcastic comments. What's next? Flying pigs?" Bri asks.

"Funny. You look nice. Deal with it. I will, however, come up with something if you don't just buy the dress and leave me alone, okay?" Sam asks with a grin.

"Got it," Bri says.

Everyone had a great day. All the girls got great dresses and actually had pains in their sides from laughing all day. It doesn't get any better than this.

CHAPTER 27

The Dance
Glitter and Good Times

Sam

The dance is tonight. Bri's more excited about my dress than I am. I didn't even bother saying I didn't want to go. Bri would win the argument just by wearing me down. Besides, even though I don't want to go, I know I have to. It feels like some kind of mile marker. Time has passed. We're older now, like it or not.

I put on some blush and lip gloss. I hate this, but if I don't, Bri will ambush me in the car. The next time I get ready like this will be for senior prom.

I look over at the picture of us from fifth-grade graduation. It was almost exactly three years ago. How can so much happen, but the time that's passed feels like a blink? How quickly will the next four years go?

My mom has come in to check on me, like, a million times. I let her do my hair. I can tell she really needs something to do. My mom looks happy to help. She's pretty amazing as moms go. My whole family is actually pretty amazing. I used to take for granted the fact that they were right there. Bri's alone so much. I've always got people there when I need them.

Sam and Bri

Sam's mom picked up Meg and Mandy and headed to Bri's. They decided that all the girls should go together. Everyone thought it would be great to have a friend thing instead of a date thing.

When we get to Bri's, no one else is home. She looks great.

"Bri, you look—" Sam is interrupted.

"Sam, you look really, really nice. I won't dwell on it, and I won't mention it again, but I don't want this night to go by without mentioning it," Bri says.

"Thanks. You would have looked nice, but you had to ruin it with all that sparkly crap. What is that glitter? Did you really put glitter on your skin?" Sam asks.

"It's body glitter. It lets you shine!"

"Like you need help shining." Sam laughs. "I just can't believe you got that junk on you all by yourself. It's kind of amazing."

"I'm glad you're impressed. Now, listen, Sam, I know you need to complain and all just to have fun, so let's get it over with. I would like to get to the fun part now," Bri says.

"Okay, ready. I just want to go on record as saying dances are stupid, these shoes are stupid, the decorations are stupid, corsages are stupid, DJs are stupid, oh, and did I mention these shoes are stupid?" Sam asks.

"Yes, I believe you did. Anything else? Did you get it all out?"

"Yup, I did, and I'm done," Sam laughs.

Sam's mom takes a bunch of pictures of them before they get in the car. Bri says her mom will be glad to see the photos.

"My mom is still having a really hard time. She can't get over this thing with my dad. It's really sad to see her like this. She used to be so different. I can't understand why she just can't move on," Bri says.

"Well," Mrs. Cooper says, "sometimes these things take time, Bri. I know it's hard, buy try to be patient with her. None of this is your fault. You're already doing everything you can. You're an amazing daughter. You do know that you are always welcome at our home. Please remember that."

"Really, Bri, anytime you need cookies, you know where to find us," Sam adds.

"Thanks," Bri says quietly, "that really means a lot."

We pull up to the school. Mrs. Barton's room has been decorated with twinkling lights. We get out of the car. Bri and Sam stop and stare at how beautiful it looks. Sam brushes a tear away.

"Are we supposed to dance at this thing or what? Why are we standing here? We look stupid!" Sam says.

"You look stupid," Bri says.

Sam pulls Bri inside and to the dance floor. The whole group danced together, one song into the next. It was like everyone was trying to hold on to the last bit of middle school. Hold on to the last bit of real childhood. It struck Bri as funny that she once thought elementary school was the end of being a kid, but now, she thought *this* was really the end of being a kid.

"Bri," Sam yells. "Hey, Bri."

"What?" Bri replies.

"I forgot to tell you that the Electric Slide is stupid." Sam laughs.

"Then why are you doing it?" Bri asks.

"'Cuz it's fun. Duh," Sam says.

The photographer came up to the group to ask them to pose for a snapshot. They all got together with arms draped around each other with great smiles on their faces. This would be what they would think of when, then would think about the dance.

CHAPTER 28

Graduation
Kids Who Stink and Their Fake Papers

Sam

We met at the school for the ceremony. My mom made a really big deal about what I was wearing and how my hair looked.

We line up alphabetically, just like we've practiced all week after finals. There was no better reward after cramming and stressing then to line up in the smelly gym and sweat with all the other sweaty people. At least I get to line up right in front of smelly Frank Costello. Frank smells so bad that if you told me he lived in a dumpster and bathed in mud and used puke perfume, I'd believe you.

So basically, I showered and got dressed in a dumb dress for my mom. Then I covered the whole thing up with this gown that weighs nine hundred pounds, then I sweated until I stunk, and then I stood in Frank's reek. So glad I shaved my legs. I look over at Bri to make myself feel better. She's right behind Delnick. He doesn't smell, but, man, that kid stinks.

Sam and Bri

Everybody sat and listened to Mr. Riley tell us how great everything in high school would be. Jack smiled with anticipation. Mr.

Riley introduced Kaitlyn, our class president. Sam turns around and tells Bri, "This should be riveting."

Bri replies, "I know, right? This will be one for the history books."

"Hey, you guys, knock it off. You're going to get in trouble. It's starting," Michael says.

Bri and Sam burst out laughing. Their noise is masked by the crowd's applause as Kaitlyn takes the podium.

"When we think back at our time at East Shore, we can all recall the best days of our lives," Kaitlyn says.

I turn to Bri. "Oh god, please tell me it gets better." Bri cracks up.

"You, guys, stop it," Delnick freaks again.

"We have to get ready for tomorrow. We have to leave behind our childish thoughts," stupid Kaitlyn says.

"Hey, Sam, do you remember standing up for freedom of expression? That was so babyish of us," Bri says.

"Yeah, what were we thinking? And the way we handled life and death, totally preschool. I wish we'd grow up," Sam says.

"You, guys, really. I can't hear." Delnick is in a complete panic now. This only makes us giggle more.

Kaitlyn is finally done and leaving the stage. We start clapping wildly. "Yay, she's done. Woohoo!" Sam yells.

Bri is clapping and laughing, wiping tears of laughter from her eyes.

Now, it's time for Mr. Riley to distribute diplomas. He calls us all to our feet to begin the procession. Just as he says, "As you move forward to meet your future," Mother Nature decides we've had enough of the ninety-four-degree temperature. She decides to coarse correct and opens up the skies with an unpredicted shower and drop in temperature.

Sam

Now, we are shivering, drenched, and Frank smells like wet dog and garbage. This is all I dreamed it would be. We get our diplomas, return to our seats, and do the throw-your-hat-in-the-air thing. This is dumb, so I don't do it. I'd rather keep my own hat for the rest of my life and not worry whose random lice-filled hat I've collected. I unscroll my diploma and it's blank.

"Why is nothing on this paper?" I ask Bri. She tells me it's just a prop. We have to go get the real one.

"I have to wait in another line to get paper after waiting in the giant line to get fake paper. I'd like to be a graduation planner when I grow up. They get to mess with people."

"You'd be good at it." Bri chuckles.

"Let's go get the real diplomas," Sam says. "I'm going to save this fake one to sell on eBay. Don't even tell me no one would want it."

"You have too much free time," Bri says.

"Or not enough. Go get your dumb real paper, and I'll see you at my house. The storm is passing. We can probably hang out outside," Sam says.

"Yeah, okay, and I, um, wanted to talk to you about something," Bri says.

"Yeah, sure, I love talking about your skirts," Sam says as she walked off onto the "C" line for her diploma.

CHAPTER 29

Sam's Backyard
Manhunt, Fireflies, and
Stories to be Developed

Sam

On the way back to my house, I realized my mother cried through the whole ceremony and the car ride home. What's wrong with her? I'm not dead or anything. Interestingly enough, the sky has stopped leaking, but my mom hasn't. Good, we'll be able to be outside.

When I got home, I immediately took off my stupid clothes and shoes and put on my normal clothes and no shoes. Everyone started showing up at the same time, all wearing their normal clothes. We went outside and sat at the picnic table, and started talking about how Kaitlyn's speech was stupid and how boring the ceremony was.

Sam and Bri

"Hey, did you guys trade your fake paper for a good one? You really need that paper. It's like a ticket to high school. If you don't have it, you don't get in," Sam jokes.

"That was pretty stupid," agrees Meg.

"You should have heard how stupid Delnick was being. He yelled at us the entire time. He was worse than the Old Miss Lee when she was still a witch," Bri adds.

"And what's up with Frank Costello? Does he actually live in a dumpster?" Jack asks.

"Standing by him is like being at the zoo in the summer," Mandy chimes in.

"My feet hurt *so* bad. I have to take these shoes off," Bri says.

Jason starts throwing the baseball around. "Hey, guys, you wanna play baseball?"

"*Ew*, why would we want to play baseball?" Bri asks. "I hate baseball."

"Baseball is stupid. Besides we are not fat enough to play baseball. Why are baseball players so fat anyway?" Sam says.

"Just shut up, Sam. Let's just play manhunt," Jay says.

"Jack, you're it!" Mandy yells, and everyone runs away.

Bri and Sam go off to hide together behind the shed. There is a loud noise followed by yelling and a lot of laughter.

"What happened?" Bri asks.

"Jack's not so nimble. He just fell over the picnic bench," Sam says.

"What? No, I mean what happened with us?" Bri says quietly.

"You disappeared and got new friends, you jerk," Sam says.

"No, my parents split up, my life fell apart, and you were nowhere to be found. I needed you, and I never heard from you all summer. You didn't even check on me," Bri says.

"Every time I saw you, you looked fine with all your new stupid friends," Sam responds.

"What do you mean? What are you talking about?" Bri asks.

"You started cheerleading, you joined every club, you started dressing like a Barbie, and acting like a teen sensation," Sam explains. "All you needed was the entourage. Oh, wait, you had one of them, didn't you?"

"I'm not talking about September. I'm talking about the whole summer. Where were you?"

"I don't know. I was working on the tree house, and you said you were going to help, and you never came. I figured you woke up and decided you hated tree houses. What was I supposed to do about that?"

"I don't know, maybe call me to see if I was okay. Why is what you're doing always the most important thing?" Bri says.

"How was I supposed to know that you were not okay? You didn't exactly put up a billboard that said *life in crisis*, did you?"

"I couldn't. I couldn't do anything. I just cried."

"I couldn't hear you crying from the treehouse, and by the way, it was a lot easier to not care. I hate worrying about people. I hate all these stupid emotions. If I knew then what I know now, I would have checked on you," Sam says.

"You should have."

"This is not just about me. What about September?" Sam says.

"Don't you get it? I had to do that! I still do! I can't be home! I hate it there! It's so sad. That's why I join everything. That's why I look like a Barbie. I can control that. People leave you alone when they think you're happy!" Bri yells.

"That's what I did. I left you alone. I didn't know! I'm not good with stuff like that. You have to say, 'I'm upset,' for me to know you're upset. I'm sorry I'm not Doctor Phil, but I really didn't know. When I started wondering where you'd been, you had already surrounded yourself with so many idiots that I couldn't get in if I tried," Sam says.

"My life, as I knew it, changed. My dad left, my mom shut down, and you forgot about me. How could you do that? You know what? I can't do this anymore. You don't care. Why should I bother?" Bri says as she storms off across the backyard.

Sam watches Bri cross the yard for a minute, then turns away. The others are moving closer now to see what the yelling is about.

"No," Sam says to herself, then louder. "No! Bri, stop. We're not doing this again." Sam starts moving toward Bri. "I do care, and you should bother because you and I are important. Remember all we did when we were on the same side? We don't like a lot of the same things. We dress different, talk different, think different, who cares? I need you in my life so I don't go crazy. I need you in my life to remind me things aren't so bad. I need you in my life to tell me I'm more than just the jerk who complains. And you need me too."

Sam is face to face with Bri now. Sam sees Bri has tears running down her cheek. "I'm sorry," Sam says. "I wish I was there for you."

"I'm sorry, too, and by the way, it's differently. We dress differently, talk differently, and think differently, not different." Bri hugs her friend until both girls find laughter through tears. The moment is broken by a loud *wap* as Jay tags Sam on the back.

"You're it," Jay says.

"Jay, are you really messing with the two people that actually staged the now-famous Paperclip Revolution? Are you insane?" Bri asks.

"How can you go out with such a stupid boy?" Sam asks Bri

"How can you not care that your feet are so muddy?" Bri asks.

"Have you looked at yours lately, Miss Perfect?" Sam asks Bri. They both look down at their feet, completely covered in mud.

The sun sets and the fireflies come out. Pure joy.

"Isn't it so pretty when the fireflies come out?" Bri asks.

"It's one of my favorite things. I still think they could be fairies," Sam says.

"You're weird," Bri says.

"I know. It's okay," Sam says.

Sam and Bri are mesmerized by the sky.

"Did you know the light is how they talk to each other?" Bri asks.

"Even fireflies have stories," Sam says.

"Everyone does. We need to remember that. We need to remember that for Mrs. Barton," Bri says.

"Hey, Bri, do you ever get freaked out about the future?" Sam asks.

"Yeah, sure. Why?" Bri replies.

"Because in a summer, we went from being friends to mortal enemies. If you and I can hate each other that fast for no good reason, then what else can change? What can we trust? What can we hold on to?" Sam wonders.

"We hold on to what Mrs. Barton told us, that everyone's story gets to turn out the way they want it to. We're still in charge, Sam. We just don't know the ending yet," Bri answers.

Sam looked around with continued wonder at this latest last day of childhood and then back up to the sky.

"It'll be really great if you're right."

Debi Cagliostro has been teaching middle school English forever. She believes we need to understand that we all have our own stories, our own versions of events. The more we read about our different stories, the more we learn empathy for our fellow humans. Being able to share these experiences with kids is why she loves teaching. She currently lives at the Jersey Shore with her husband and two teenage children.

Beth A. Lee has been teaching middle school English since 2013. She believes putting books in kids' hands is one of the most powerful ways to better the world. Teaching a student to express themselves is the most rewarding job known to man. She currently lives at the Jersey Shore with her two daughters.

Debi and Beth met in 2009 when Debi was her eldest daughter's seventh-grade English teacher.

CPSIA information can be obtained
at www.ICGtesting.com
Printed in the USA
LVHW031354311220
675393LV00006B/1011